THE FIRST CHRISTMAS

ABOUT THE AUTHOR

Michael Mullen was born in Castlebar in County Mayo. He was educated in Waterford and at University College, Dublin. He has published many books for adults and children, including the bestselling *The Hungry Land*. He is particularly interested in writing for young people and *The First Christmas* is his eighth children's book for Poolbeg.

THE FIRST CHRISTMAS

MICHAEL MULLEN

Children's
POOLBEG

First published in 1993 by
Poolbeg,
A division of Poolbeg Enterprises Ltd,
Knocksedan House,
Swords, Co. Dublin, Ireland

A catalogue record for this book is available from the British Library.

ISBN 1 85371 296 5

Cover illustration by Marie Louise Fitzpatrick
Cover design by Poolbeg Group Services Ltd
Set by Mac Book Limited in Stone 12/17
Printed by The Guernsey Press Limited,
Vale, Guernsey, Channel Islands.

For Jim and Maureen Donahue

Contents

1

The Crib

It was a crisp night. The frost was deep. It had formed crusted patterns on the windows and the village Christmas lights made a blurred and beautiful picture on the panes. Daniel had been reading the Christmas story in a old book he had discovered in the attic. Shepherds and kings marched across the faded pages and in an arch across each page were pictured the stars and that great star that had guided the kings through ribbed sands, across vast deserts and by green oases to the cave in Bethlehem. His eyes were tired with the wonder.

He knuckled his eyes and softened the lids,

then left the small desk at which he had been sitting and went to the the window. In order to see what was happening below on the the village green, he rubbed away the patterned glaze of frost. He could hear the voices of men calling to each other. Among them he recognised the voice of his friend, John Duffy, the local carpenter, who was in control of the whole confused drama. His shop was at the edge of the village green. Had he kept to his trade he could have made a lot of money. Instead he painted pictures and carved statues from wood. These were packed away at the back of his workshop like actors waiting to appear on stage.

Daniel unlocked the window and pushed it out. The air was sharp. A white fog lay about and above the village green and through it figures moved in a mysterious fashion. Now and then the mist would part and reveal them more clearly; then it would close again.

Among them he recognised John Duffy, clad in his loose dungarees. He was in charge of the crib. A frieze of men and children were carrying the sections from his shop. It was that time of year when John Duffy became fully important.

Daniel looked in wonder as the scene unfolded itself beneath him on the stiff grass. The back of the crib was set up, showing the imagined hills and hollows of Bethlehem. Then the sides, showing other hills, were slotted in. Finally the great frame was set in place and the wonder of Bethlehem was there on the village green.

John Duffy enjoyed his role as crib-builder. Standing in his paint-spattered dungarees he directed the men as they assembled the structure and then walked around the great square box and examined it. When he was satisfied, he directed his helpers to bring out the carved figures. He had done so much carving over the years that the crib had become very crowded.

"We must follow the story," he argued, when others questioned his judgement.

He was a heavy shapeless man who looked comfortable only in loose dungarees which even then strained at the double-stitched seams. On his way home from school, Daniel often called into his workshop, so full of the smell of wood and glue. It looked confused and chaotic: there seemed neither order nor rule to the place. Wood chippings curled in dry heaps on the floor. Planks of timber ranging in colour from silver whites to dark browns stood slanted against the walls. There was always some unfinished piece of work close to the door.

"I am an artist, Daniel," John often re-marked. "If they want windows and doors made, why don't they go elsewhere. I want only to carve statues and figures—make something of value out of wood. When I see an oak log I see a figure inside it, crying to get out." Daniel was one of the few people who was ever permitted to visit John's workshop and observe him at work. John explained to him the secrets of his trade. He never began to carve until his chisels were set out in order, ranging from the fine-bladed ones which were for delicate work to the large ones which did the rough shaping.

"You must follow the grain, follow the grain," he observed as he worked on the seasoned wood. "I know carpenters who destroy wood; they work against the grain."

Sometimes Daniel sat and watched him work. No words might pass between them for half an hour. Small sounds filled the silence: the crackle of wood pieces in the belly-shaped stove, the scurry of mice, wind whistling through a chink.

"You have a clear mind," he often told Daniel, "It is filled with wonder. Don't let anyone destroy your imagination."

Daniel did not know what John meant. He only knew that when he entered the workshop, his mind was entranced and he did not feel time passing by.

The carpenter had a wonderful store of books in his house which was beside the workshop. Sometimes he brought one to Daniel and urged him to read it. "There is something there which might interest you," he would say. There always was.

Now Daniel gazed at the people gathered on the green. The great moment had arrived. He could hear their voices with a bell-like clarity. Soon the doors of the carpenter's shop would be opened and the figures carried to the green. He wondered what new figure would be added to those about the crib this year.

Soon the first figure emerged—a Roman soldier with a tunic of leather, a helmet bearing an eagle and his short sword by his side. It was carried by four men.

"What has a Roman soldier to do with the Christmas story?" someone asked.

"He has plenty to do with the story, but I am not going to argue about it," the carpenter replied gruffly as he walked behind them, his hands deep in his dungaree pockets.

The Roman soldier was set in place. The men and boys gathered about and gazed at him. He seemed familiar.

"He's very like the sergeant," one of them said.

"It's Sergeant Cummins, sure enough. He has his big nose and the wart on the chin," another remarked.

They asked the carpenter about the likeness but he was not forthcoming.

The second figure was small and burly, with a round face and heavy jowls. He too was given his place beside the crib.

He resembled the local hotel owner. This too was remarked upon.

"All characters and events in this crib are from the Christmas story and any resemblance to living characters is entirely accidental," John Duffy replied.

There were always the same questions at Christmastime and they were always answered in the same fashion. This was one of the pleasures in being at the unveiling.

Other figures were brought from the carpenter's shop, so that soon the crib was crowded with figures. They were made to stretch down the road into the heart of the small town of Bethlehem. This was only the beginning of things. Figures were added until finally, on Christmas night, the sacred family would be placed in the cave, which now stood empty.

The lights were switched on. The crib became a theatre. To give it authenticity somebody suggested that a tape recorder should be installed in the straw. But the carpenter would not hear of such a thing.

"No! That far I will not go. Something must be left to the imagination."

Eventually the crowds left the green with obvious reluctance. They disappeared into the swirling fog. But some of the towns-people returned later to study their own images in the crib.

When it was late, the sergeant made his rounds. He walked across the green and looked into the crib. He was quite pleased. He represented the law not only in the village but also in Bethlehem.

Daniel felt the town grow quiet. People came out of the pubs and made their way in the various directions that lead from the village. Lights went on in bedrooms and then went off. Periodically a car drove through the village, its headlights sweeping about the crescent and then passing onwards into the darkness.

It grew colder. The frost was silvery grey and the grass crisp and brittle.

Daniel decided he must see the crib. He had watched the carpenter fashion the figures and he wished to see them in place.

He waited until the house was quiet. His father and mother had retired to bed and his brothers and sisters were asleep across the corridor. Quietly he dressed and put on his warm duffle-coat. Then he slipped out of the room, padded down the stairs and entered the kitchen, taking care not to knock a tin or pot to the floor. He unlocked the door. It creaked as he opened. Soon he was in the frost-hardened lane. He stumbled through the darkness and twice   nearly lost his balance on patches of ice.

The cold was intense and lonely. But he felt warm because he was excited. He moved up through the archway. He looked up and down the street. The village was empty. He crossed the road to the green. The ground was hard and white. He came to the crib and looked at it in awe and wonder. It was the best the carpenter had ever created. He moved closer. The figures within seemed alive.

Daniel looked about him. There was nobody in sight. The village was asleep. He entered the crib.

His adventure was about to begin.

2

A Cold Night in Bethlehem

It was cold in Bethlehem. A wind blew from the shallow hills to the south. Above the town the night sky was crusted with stars. They seemed to pulse with life.

Daniel found himself at the end of a street. Most of the buildings were square and squat, though some were quite large. A group of men wearing coloured robes stood about a fire warming themselves. The flames from the fire lit their shadowy faces. They were talking quietly. Daniel stood in the shadows and listened to their conversation.

"This census will make you rich, Jaban,"

one of the men remarked. "You will have to bake extra loaves. Why, today I saw many strangers ride into town from the north. They were rich by their appearance. Merchants and their families, I would say. Of the house of David, I'd say. They come to Bethlehem from every corner of the world and must have seen wonders on their travels."

"Perhaps," Jaban the baker replied. "Praise the Lord it has been a good year for me. There were years when I barely made a living."

"I have never known a baker to be poor," one of the group remarked, "and even if he is poor he will not starve."

"I pay my taxes to the Romans. That leaves me poor. What man in Bethlehem is rich?"

"The innkeeper, Ben," came the reply. "The merchants passing through stable their camels in his great courtyard and they pay well for their comforts."

"There is no equality on this earth. The poor remain poor and the rich grow richer every day," a young man said. "The Romans impose a heavy burden upon us. We need someone who will save us. We need a leader we can follow, a leader such as David and Solomon were. We have fallen upon bad days." His eyes flashed as he spoke.

"But is it not written in the Sacred Book that this saviour of our nation will be born at Bethlehem?" urged Jaban. "He will be another David who will lead us against the Romans and the old kingdom will be established again."

"So I have heard," an old man commented.

"We will rise up and be free," the young man added.

"You talk too much, Simon. If Sixtus the Roman centurion hears such talk he will have you sent in chains to Jerusalem. You might disappear into Herod's dungeon and never be seen again. Much worse, they could pluck out your eyes and send you wandering the roads of Judea as a beggar. Evil things happen in Jerusalem."

The company fell silent. They heard the

steps of Sixtus as he made his rounds. He was in charge of the town garrison. It was his business to keep a watchful eye on the place and report back to his superiors in Jerusalem.

But there was little to report. Except at the time of the census nothing much happened in the sleepy town.

Sixtus approached the fire. He was wearing his leather tunic and lorica. At his side he carried his short sword. He carried his helmet. His hair was short and grey and he had a muscular neck. A scar ran down his left cheek. He had been on many campaigns and knew much of the world. He was a man of fifty but could still march that number of miles in a day if necessary. He often stopped at the fire on this way about the town.

"Goodnight, neighbours," he began, "I feel that we will have snow."

"Ay. That we will. The wind has shifted," one of the men replied.

"Then it will be cold on the hills. The shepherds will have to be wary of wolves. They will be on the prowl. I heard them howling last night."

"They are not the only wolves in Bethlehem," Simon remarked, his hatred for the Roman presence evident in his voice.

"You have a loose tongue, Simon," said Sixtus with a patient smile. "It will get you into trouble some day. My tour here will soon be at an end and I will return with my men to Rome. Another will take my place who may not be as lenient as I am. Keep your rebellious thoughts to yourself. Herod has spies everywhere. All I want is peace and quiet!"

For a moment there was tension about the fire. Simon was a hot-headed young man and could be a dangerous companion.

"How many strangers came today?" asked one of the men, in order to break the silence.

"Thirty. The inns are crowded. Last night the guard was called upon to prevent a quarrel. It was about a fine point in your scriptures. I could not follow the arguments. I disarmed the men and let them off with a warning. Let us hope that these people arriving in Bethlehem will keep the peace.

But I must be on my way…Goodnight."

With that he turned and walked down the ill-lit street. The men waited until he was out of earshot. One of them turned to Simon.

"Keep your tongue under control. Sixtus is the best Roman officer who has been stationed here. He is a reasonable man. Another would have thrown you in prison or, worse still, run you through with a sword. Leave well enough alone."

The others agreed. The land was at peace. They did not wish for trouble. Simon, perhaps wisely, was silent.

Daniel listened to the conversation for a while longer. Then he decided to explore the little town. He felt at home in the place and the men gathered around the fire had taken his presence for granted. Perhaps they thought that he was one of the strangers from the inn. He walked down towards the communal well. The town was a compact place. Alleyways ran from the street that was the continuation of the road to Jerusalem. As he ventured down one, he could hear people talking in some of the little houses. Most houses were in darkness because of the hour.

Daniel wandered through the maze of alleyways and soon he was lost. Then he heard the sound of strange music. He decided to find out where it came from and it led him to a large building near the centre of the town. It was the largest inn in this city of David; it towered over the other buildings. A row of windows ran along the top and bright lights burned in many of them. The great door leading to the inner courtyard was slightly open. Daniel moved over and peeped in. In the centre a great fire blazed. Ringed about it were magnificent cushions and carpets. Men in rich robes sat around, impervious to the cold. Several men were dancing about the fire, while close by two musicians played on instruments he did not recognise. The place was rich with strange aromas, different from any he had ever smelled before. He drew a deep breath. They filled his nostrils with pleasure.

It was obvious that these were the rich

merchants of whom the men who had sat about the brazier had spoken. Along the walls stood their camels. They were great rough-haired beasts. They snorted deeply and spat, showing their teeth under rubbery lips. Set in the wall of the courtyard were glowing lanterns. Figures moved quietly along the colonnades. Daniel crouched in the shadow of the wall, his mind engrossed but with a certain fear in his heart. If he were caught he might be taken before the innkeeper and asked all sorts of unanswerable questions.

Suddenly he heard a boy scream.

"No, master, I did not steal the dates. Honestly. I am a poor boy trying to make a few mites for my mother."

"Then go to where the camels are stabled and water them."

"Very well, sir. Consider it done, sir," the boy cried as if in pain. There was a final squeal and the young boy was thrown through the door and landed at Daniel's feet. He picked himself up nimbly.

"Are you all right?" Daniel asked

anxiously.

"Of course I'm all right. Trust Seth to take care of himself. The louder I roar the more Ben the innkeeper enjoys it. So I roar. But I *have* dates. They are brought here by the merchants and here is a special sweetmeat brought all the way from Turkey." He put his hand in his tunic and drew out a bundle.

The two boys sat on a wooden seat and began to munch the dates and the Turkish delight. Seth was small, with bright, intelligent eyes. He munched rapidly on the dates and sweets, obviously enjoying them.

"You come with me and you will be safe. I know my way around this town. Four times Sixtus the Roman soldier followed me through the streets and four times he got lost. I keep away from him. He warned my mother that he would throw me in prison. But I am not afraid."

"Seth," a voice roared. "You come right here and serve the gentlemen wine."

"Ben's wife. If Ben is not calling Ben's wife is calling. You come with me. I will say that you are a relation come for the census. Chances are you will get a job here."

They entered a large storeroom. It was filled with all types of delicious food and had to be guarded each night. Honey and wines were stored in glazed jars. Fine pastries stood on trays and dried fruits were heaped on brown dishes.

"Who have you got there, Seth?" Liz the servant woman, asked.

"A relative from Gaza," he lied.

"Never known you to have a relation in the whole wide world," Ruth said.

"Well I got one in Gaza. Never knew I had until he turned up for the census."

"I hope that he is a better worker than you, for I believe, Seth, that you are up to all sorts of tricks. Your mind is always set on stealing. I keep my eye fixed on you and you take things straight from under my eye. Never knew one like you, Seth. Now you and your friend can go and serve the merchants from Egypt some wine. And don't spill it on their garments. They're made from the finest cloth."

She was a small fat woman, with a full olive-coloured face and a pleasant expression. Her hair was black and lustrous and hung down her back.

She gave them two silver jugs of wine. Daniel was a little anxious.

"Don't worry; just do what I do," Seth told him reassuringly.

They left the larder and walked out into the courtyard, going straight to the open space right next to the fire where the merchants lay on soft cushions and carpets.

"Wines for the finest gentlemen. Wines for the fine gentlemen," Seth called out in an important voice.

The merchants held up their goblets and Seth poured out measures of wine. He moved nimbly among the reclining figures. Daniel followed him and tried to imitate his gestures.

"What is your name?" a thin merchant with a dried face asked.

"I am Seth of Bethlehem," he said

proudly.

"A descendant of David no doubt."

"Yes, sir. I am proud of my line."

"And is it from your family the king will come?" the merchant asked with a laugh.

"So it is written. So my master at the synagogue tells us."

"You believe this nonsense?"

"I do, sir."

Seth was angry but he restrained his tongue. This merchant was not one of his people. He did not know the scriptures. He was an Egyptian who passed through Bethlehem once a year. It was said that he was also a thief and a murderer. Seth had heard whispers that he had killed merchants in the desert and left their bones bleaching under the hot sun. There was the look of evil in his eyes. Seth moved quickly away from his presence.

The traders from the north were men of wealth. They did not have to make journeys through the long stretches of the southern desert. They travelled with escorts of servants and soldiers. They lived in the privileged places to the north, where the wind was perfumed and gentle on the skin. They wore soft robes and rubbed their bodies with perfumed oil.

"You dance for me, Seth," one of them commanded. "I am tired of the others."

"Not only shall I dance, sir, but I shall juggle while I dance," he replied.

Seth took three oranges from a plate. He steadied himself and began to juggle. Then he began to dance. It was a funny little dance he had invented and it drew roars of laughter from the crowd. All would have gone well had not one of the Egyptians tripped him so that he fell forward on to the ground. The oranges fell on his head and the crowd began to laugh uproariously. Seth picked himself up. There were tears in his eyes but he suppressed them. He began to smile and returned to the shadows.

"These Egyptians are scum!" he hissed to Daniel, "but I must not lose my temper. Ben would throw me on to the street and my mother would have to go without food if I lost my job." He sighed and made Daniel feel sorry for him. However the lad quickly recovered his good humour.

Meanwhile the talk continued about the great fire. Meat was roasting on a spit. It filled the courtyard with its aroma. For those who had travelled across the great deserts and come through barren places this meal was like manna from heaven. Ben moved amongst the rich merchants, making certain that they were comfortable and well served. He considered himself a most fortunate man. God had truly blessed him. He had worked hard and had built up the fame of his inn. It had prospered. His name was known even in the great city of Jerusalem. The priests made a fuss of him when he entered Solomon's temple to pray. He presented them with costly gifts each year when he travelled to the sacred city. Now his wife was expecting their first child. Every blessing had been showered upon him.

"You, Seth," Ben called. "Tell the gatekeeper to close the outer gates. I cannot accept further guests. The rooms have been reserved by the merchants. They pay double for their comforts."

"You come with me to the gatekeeper, Gideon," said Seth. He takes too much grog for his own good but he has a good heart."

They slipped along by the arched courtyard.

Gideon was sitting in a small hut, a cloak wrapped about his shoulders.

"Time to close the gates, Gideon. The master says that the merchants have rented all the rooms. They do not wish to have the riff-raff of the place disturbing their feast."

"And where will the descendants of David sleep if there is no room at the inn or in the houses? Already there is no room in the houses but there are still plenty of rooms in the inn."

"That is the order, Gideon."

"And Gideon obeys orders. He has always obeyed orders. He obeys the Romans and he obeys the priests and he obeys Ben and he obeys the laws of Moses. Gideon sometimes got tired of obeying laws and not being his own man. I wish I was my own man. Yes, I do wish I was my own man," he sighed.

"Tell us a story, Gideon," Seth pleaded.

"No night for a story. It is too cold and my old bones are frozen."

"What if you had a goblet of wine?" Seth asked.

"That might make a difference."

Seth disappeared into the shadows and returned with a goblet of wine.

"You be careful of the law, Seth, or you will end up in jail. Did you steal this vessel?" Gideon asked.

"I borrowed it. There happened to be wine inside."

"You're just like the priests up in Jerusalem. Splitting words. They split words until they don't have a meaning any more. Words mean something, words don't mean nothing."

He began to drink the wine.

"You ever heard of Job?" he asked after he had supped the wine.

"No," Seth lied.

"You sure?"

"We're sure." Seth answered imitating the old man's way of speaking.

"He had to put up with lots of trouble, that man Job. I heard about him when I was growing up. I heard the whole story right as it happened. He had some good times at the beginning but then he had a heap of bad times. He was once high and then he was low. They told me that he had once to sit on a dungheap, he was so low."

The boys sat in awe while Gideon told the story of Job. It was full of local interest and colour and came alive to them. Seth had been warned at the synagogue not to listen to Gideon. He made up his own proverbs and said that they were to be found in the Bible. He was regarded by the elders as a bad influence on children.

While they listened to the story the feast continued behind them. Now that the fatted calves had been roasted on the spit, the rich tender meat was carved and presented to the merchants. That ate the fine food contentedly.

Night advanced about the inn. The stars grew more brilliant. The cold, held at bay by the great fires, now descended upon the courtyard. The merchants, satisfied, retired to deep and comfortable beds. The servants moved about the courtyard and gathered the plates and vessels and the remnants of the food.

Gideon said goodbye to Seth and Daniel when they were finished their chores. He let them out through the small door in the great gate. They walked down the dark street of Bethlehem. Somewhere in the cold distance a wolf howled and they shivered. They moved quickly, passing by the Roman garrison where an oil lamps still burned. They passed down an alleyway where the very poor of Bethlehem lived. Seth arrived at his home, which was just one small room. A curtain divided the living space. Seth whispered that they should not disturb his mother. On tip-toe, Daniel found the bed. It was a carpet and upon it lay rough blankets. Too tired to feel uncomfortable, Daniel lay down to sleep in Bethlehem. It had been an exciting night and he was exhausted. Quickly he drifted down into sleep and dreams.

3

The Magi

They had seen the star in their homeland in the east. That had been nine months before. It had stood above the desert, a new star amongst the old. It had appeared on the night that Caspar had stood watch on the great tower with his servants. He was the chief of the priest-astronomers and his knowledge of the heavens was immense. It was believed that he knew the name of each star on the great arch of night.

The Magi often recalled the night of that first sighting as they made the long journey across the great and hostile desert. Wrapped in his warm priestly cloak on the great tower, Casper had studied the sky. Here and there comets arched across the sky and after a brief life died, it seemed, on the desert edge. It was an ordinary night and the magus was about to abandon his watch when he noted an expanding glow to the west. He watched in fascination as the nova grew and began to pulse. A halo of light surrounded it. Caspar looked on in awe. It grew in size. He thought perhaps that it might explode and cast a shower of lesser stars across the sky. Then it ceased to throb and settled into a firm glow. A new star had been born. He continued to gaze at the new body in the sky. Perhaps it would fail and fall back into the darkness out of which it had sprung. But it held its strength and took its place in the firmament.

"Quickly go in search of Melchior and Balthasar," Caspar said to one of the attendants. He must inform the other Magi. He knew the importance of the new star. It had been prophesied in the sacred books of the Parsee.

The servant hastened down the long curved staircases which connected the platforms of the observatory. When he reached the bottom he ran through the town until he reached the houses of Melchior. He, too, was excited at the event. He rushed into the great hall, shouting to the servants, "Tell your master Melchior that a new star has appeared in the west."

There was a great flurry of excitement as Melchior put on his woollen robes and prepared to go to the observatory. The same excitement filled the house of Balthasar. He was the eldest of the Magi and had a very long thin face and a small fine beard. His eyes showed the signs of much peering at the heavens.

"Is it true? It did not shoot across the desert and die in the sand?"

"No. It grew into a sun and we thought perhaps that it might explode. But it shrank back into the size of a large star and now hangs high in the western sky."

"This exceeds expectation. All the stars I

know, indeed I have named many. But a new star is a strange event. It marks the coming of a king. It has been written of in our great books. But we must hasten. Quickly, take me to the tower.

He moved slowly out of the house, for he was a great age and his bones were brittle. They placed him on a pallet and brought him to the base of the observatory. There the servants lifted him on their strong shoulders and carried him up the stairs to the highest platform.

All Balthasar's life had been devoted to a study of the stars. On clay tablets and papyrus scrolls that were preserved in the great library he had read the observations of former priests. He had written down his own comments and printed them on clay tablets which had been baked firm and stored in the library. Now it would be his duty to describe and name the new star.

Caspar was standing at the great stone table upon which representations of the night skies had been chiselled. It was a huge circle and contained the positions of all the visible stars. They had been set in segments of thirteen and corresponded with the lunar months of the year.

Balthasar sat on a priestly throne and gazed at the new star which shone in the west. His old heart began to beat excitedly. The three Magi had often spoken of such a possibility.

"It certainly means that a new king is born. We must follow this star and see where it will take us," he urged.

"But are you not too old for such a journey? Can you bear the heat of the burning sun by day and the freezing air by night?" Caspar and Melchior asked anxiously.

"I *am* an old man now. My life is running out but for all of that life I have hoped for such an event. I will go! Let us make preparations for this journey."

They descended the tower and went to the house of Melchior, who was the most travelled amongst them, he had been to visit the astronomers of Egypt. Sitting before a wooden table on which he had etched the map of his wanderings, he explained the time and the distances the journey would take.

"We must allow ourselves a year or perhaps two. There are many wonders on the way which we must see and many cities which we may visit."

They called their household supervisors, men of great experience. Not only did these stewards take charge of the household but they trained the servants in the use of arms. The Magi explained what plans they had in mind. The stewards calculated how much it would cost and how long it would take to prepare for the journey: they were chosen for their wisdom as well as their courage.

Next day there was much excitement in the city. The three Magi who were in charge of the king's tower had discovered a new star in the western sky. It presaged the birth of a child who would be a king. Perhaps too it was the promise of a good year. The crops watered by the Tigris canals would run with fresh water and feed the thirsty wheat fields. These great canals were the blood-vessels of the land. The stars were the messengers of the gods, foretelling both good times and times of ill-fortune.

It took the Magi three weeks to prepare the camel train. A party of thirty would travel through the fertile lands and inhospitable deserts. Every item need for the journey had been listed on waxed tablets with styluses of bronze. The great humped beasts with nodding heads and filthy breaths cried out in the courtyard as they were tackled for the journey. Each camel was checked for tents, carpets, gifts, money and weapons. They would travel for five months through friendly and fertile countries, spending a day and a night at the astral towers which were dotted across the territory of the king. But beyond the limits of the fertile land fed by the canals lay unknown dangers.

They set off before the break of dawn. Zenos, the most experienced of the servants, led the way. The stars were still in the sky and the sun had not yet begun to light the eastern sky. The Magi mounted their camels. They followed their guides and servants out through the town gates.

Five months later they had reached the limits of the kingdom. They had passed through a land of plenty where all was settled and ordered. The earth was fertile. Fruit trees were carefully tended and there was always the scent of perfume on the air.

They passed through the fabled land of flowers and honey. It seemed to stretch endlessly to the horizon. They plucked flowers whose names they did not know. At night they fell asleep with languid perfume filling their nostrils. They were drugged by the perfume and the matchless beauty of the place. They drank the golden honey of Datar with their wine as they relaxed in their tents.

Later they entered a land of herbs and wine. Here in wooden buildings the herbs were laid out to dry. Each herb had some medicinal property. They were sent to the cities of the kingdom to cure the ill and ease the ailing. The chief herbalist, who had lived all his life in the valley, brought them through the fields. He explained to them the properties of a thousand herbs whose names they could not possibly remember. Before they left he presented them with several small satchels of herbs. On the leather flaps were stamped their names and their properties.

"You may need them in the lands beyond the desert," he advised them.

They noted everything they saw. Later they would record their new knowledge on tablets and scrolls and set them in the library so that others might benefit from their knowledge.

And now the desert lay ahead. They would travel directly west. The desert marked the boundary between the Roman Empire and the kingdom of Parthia. Their route lay through the town of Aleppo. Their trek would be across a dangerous expanse of desert, with the likelihood of sudden storms blowing up from the west. The desert could be merciless.

They reached the small outpost of Ahrab six months after the beginning of their journey. It was a long finger of land running out into the desert. Here in the twisted streets amongst flat-roofed houses the scum of the region lived furtive lives. Many had fled across the desert from Roman law. Others, known criminals in the east, were preparing to cross the desert. Every night someone died in Ahrab. The Valley of Picked Bones lay some distance from the town. The vultures circled this hollow slowly, silently with bald necks, waiting for their prey.

Arsaches was ruler of Ahrab. Zenos paid a call on him. He lived in a massive fort guarded by his soldiers. Like himself, they were ruthless men, dressed in rough robes and armed to the teeth, who never relaxed their vigilance.

"What brings wise men to this place? Have they not a soft and pleasant life by the Euphrates, the father of rivers. Have we stars here that are not seen on the great towers which stand throughout their land?"

"We seek a guide who will take us through the desert," Zenos replied. "We wish to cross to Aleppo. We would pay well for him."

Arsaches looked closely at Zenos. He could not determine his race. He could have been from Egypt. Or perhaps further south in the land of Africa. He had black skin, a bald head and bright, intelligent eyes. He carried a sword and was supple in his movements: a man dangerous to challenge to swordplay.

"To the west lies the land of the Romans. The customs and the manners are different. They obey different laws. What leads you to such a foreign place?"

"The birth of a new king," he replied.

"Then this king may some day become emperor, perhaps rule the Roman world. In which province of the empire will he be born?"

"We follow a star. It will take us there," Zenos stated simply. He looked warily at Arsaches. He was sure he could not be trusted.

"I will hire out my best guides to you," said the wily chieftain. "They will show you the way across the desert. In return you will give me four pieces of gold."

"Very well," he said. "We intend to depart before sunrise."

He returned to the caravanserai and quickly organised the camels and caravans into a ring. Behind the ring he set armed servants and instructed them: "Watch carefully. This is an evil place. There is no goodness here and no mercy to be shown."

All that night they stood guard. The town never slept. In a tavern close by, there was a brawl. A dead traveller was thrown on to the street. Raucous singing continued throughout the night.

Very early the guides arrived. Zenos studied them. They were from the shore of the Euxine Sea. Their only weapons were daggers and they were already dressed in long desert robes. They rode scrawny camels.

"Follow us," they said sullenly. "We will lead you to Aleppo."

The train moved out into the desert. When the sun rose the great expanse became a furnace. The camels moved to the rhythm of the desert, nodding their heads mechanically. Towards midday the heat was intense. The travellers bivouacked in the desert and and slept in what shade the camels could provide. At evening when the first stars were showing they set out again. They were three days into the desert when they reached the first well. It was dry. By now their water supply was running low.

The guides looked at the sandy waterhole. "We must ride to the top of the sand-dunes and find our bearings," one of them said.

While the party rested by the empty well the guides made their way to the top of the dune. They disappeared from sight. The Magi became suspicious. "Find these fellows and bring them here," they ordered.

But the servants could not find them. They had disappeared. The travellers had been abandoned to the menace of the burning, empty sands. It was obvious that they had been led into a trap. It was intended that they should die from thirst.

Zenos gazed at the sky. It was approaching midday and the burning sun beat down upon them. If they were to continue further they would get lost, perhaps hallucinate and wander about in circles until they died. Arsaches would send his men to steal their treasures. "Let us set up our tents and rest. We cannot move further for the moment. We would quickly die of thirst. I think I have a plan that may save us," Zenos told them.

The sun wheeled to the west and shadows grew longer. Darkness fell. Zenos studied the stars. He came to a decision. "Now we will release some of the camels. They will smell water and lead us to some wadi or oasis. I can find our bearings from the stars and I know the general direction in which Aleppo lies."

The Magi mounted their camels and followed the camels that had been released. For a moment they sniffed the cool night air. Then they moved forward, as if guided by some instinct.

All that night the group travelled south-west. As morning broke over the desert a great oasis appeared on the horizon. They moved towards it hoping that it might not be a desert mirage. Soon they realised that it was a place where great palm-trees grew, where water bubbled out of the earth into wells and where they could rest and fodder their animals.

That night they took their bearings. They were south of their course. But with leather bags filled with precious water and their camels rested, they set off north towards Aleppo and the Roman world.

4

Herod

Jerusalem was quiet. Herod looked down on the great city from one of the towers of his palace. He had wrapped himself in a thick woollen cloak against the cold. As he grew older the cold seemed to cut deeper into his bones. He had restored Jerusalem as he had restored many other cities in his kingdom. He had built in stone and in the Roman style. It was a beautiful city of which he felt proud.

"It was a city of rubble and ruins before I set to work upon it," he often boasted to his secretary, Janus.

But Herod had never been accepted by

the Jews. His mother had been an Arabian princess and so his blood was tainted. The priests and others said that he was lukewarm in the practice of religion and paid only lip-service to the Jewish laws.

He prided himself upon his watch-fulness: "It is because I notice small details that the kingdom is at peace. If there is to be a rebellion it will start somewhere on the edge of my kingdom and not in Jerusalem. Some prophet may come up from the desert and stir up the people. You must be alert," he told his soldiers.

But recently he was becoming suspicious of everybody. His own household was against him. His children wondered whom he would appoint as his successor. He had little mercy on those who moved against him or threatened his throne. Two of his sons he had executed because they had planned to overthrow him. They were the sons of Miriamne, the granddaughter of Hyrcanus II. When he married Miriamne he had married well and advanced his ambitions. He now ruled a wide and peaceful kingdom. Augustus Caesar, the first emperor of Rome, had supported him in all his actions. Herod had ensured that there was no breach of the peace during his reign. For this reason Herod was well respected in Rome and had many friends at the imperial city.

He was particularly pleased with the state of Jerusalem during the census period. Jews were arriving from all over the Middle East to be registered. They had tasted the delights and the civilisation of the Roman world and they appreciated Herod's taste. His fame was carried across the Mediterranean, even to Rome itself.

"The native Jews are backward," he remarked to Janus, his secretary of thirty years.

"They are not part of the Roman empire," replied the secretary. "They are a conquered race. But in their hearts they are not conquered. They read their scriptures and draw confidence and hope from them. You know what they expect: another David or Solomon who will lead them to glory. But we live in a modern world and not a world of little local tribes. They may be backward but they must be watched. This belief that a king will be born from among them is a dangerous notion. I listen to the talk..."

"And do you believe it, Janus?" Herod asked.

"It matters not what I believe," Janus answered astutely. "It is what the masses believe that has to be considered."

Herod looked at the old man. He was thin and spare with a gaunt face. He never spoke out of turn and seemed to be always close at hand. He slept little but spent his nights working on documents. Herod knew that despite his humble demeanour he had a sharp mind and was one of the few people he could trust.

A servant made his way on to the battlements. He stood quietly until he was summoned. "Well? What news do you bring?" Herod asked.

"Some merchants from the north have

arrived in the city. They request an audience with you. They bear rich gifts."

"I will see them in the public room," Herod directed.

He looked once more at the city which he had restored. Then he descended from the towers to the chamber, which was pleasantly furnished in the Roman fashion. Mosaics covered the floor. In the corner a brazier burned. His chair of state, carved from cedar of Lebanon, stood on a dais half-way down one side of the ornate room.

The merchants entered. They were rich men. This was clear from their fine clothes and their retinue. They were men of taste and intelligence and had come from the trading cities in the north. Herod approached the throne, accompanied by four soldiers dressed in Roman armour. His guards impressed visitors and were also protection against would-be assassins. Twice his life had been in danger. Once, as he walked through a crowd gathered about the temple, they had grown angry and called him a renegade. His soldiers had forced a path through the angry mob. But a zealot, waving a dagger, had burst through the cordon. Before he could plunge the blade into Herod's heart a bodyguard had drawn his sword and killed him.

"You fool," Herod had said to the guard later on, after they had returned to his fortress. "You should have taken him alive. Perhaps he is part of a conspiracy. He did not act alone, I can assure you." He was always conscious of such dangers. Even in his own palace he felt he was no longer safe. There he did not fear the sword or the dagger; he feared the poisoners.

The merchants bowed when he entered. He took his seat and begged them to speak.

The opening address was one of praise for Herod, which pleased him greatly. The merchants expressed their admiration for the manner in which he had improved the city.

"The water is as pure and clear as that which springs up in the desert," the leader commented.

Herod enjoyed such praise.

"And the temple you have built for the Jews is one of the wonders of Jerusalem. This we were told by those who visited us in the north. Your fame is great throughout the east."

When the chief merchant was finished, he ordered his servants to advance and present gifts to Herod. One long ornamental box contained a jewelled sword. Another servant presented him with a bale of fine silk brought from the very outer regions of the world. A third presented him with a necklace of precious amber.

"And how can I reward such generosity?" he asked.

"We would like to open trade routes with Egypt. Jerusalem would be central to our plan. Here we could build or rent large depots and have a resting place for our camels."

"I see. Of course that would mean that I would have to place my soldiers at your disposal. You would need protection. It can be expensive."

"We understand. We are willing to pay

for such protection. We have agreed upon a certain sum. Would a thousand gold pieces be sufficient as an annual payment?" the leader suggested.

Herod looked at this soft-faced merchant. His eyes were still, even innocent.

"Three thousand gold pieces would be a more realistic price," Herod replied.

"Very well, your majesty. Three thousand gold pieces. We will pay in advance."

The chief merchant snapped his fingers. Two servants bowed and left the room. Some time later they returned with a chest which they placed it at the feet of Herod.

The merchant moved forward and opened the lid. Herod looked at the glittering coins of gold.

"There are three thousand gold coins here for your majesty. We are honourable men."

"And if I had asked for ten thousand coins what would you have done?" Herod asked.

"We understand that you are a reasonable king, a king that merchants can do business with," the merchant answered blandly.

Herod smiled at the merchant who could judge him so closely.

"Where do you travel to for the census?" he asked.

"Bethlehem."

"Then you are almost there. If you wish you may stay at one of my palaces in the city. In the morning you can set out, inscribe your names on the register and return. There is little of interest in Bethlehem," he said.

"Our family came from Bethlehem. We wish to return there. We are of the house of David."

There was a certain firm pride in his voice as he spoke. The pride annoyed Herod but he concealed his feelings. These Jews felt royal blood flow in their veins. They believed in the prophecies. They believed in their Messiah.

When they had left the palace Herod

turned to his secretary. "Why do men brought up in the world of Rome, who follow our laws and speak the Latin tongue, believe in these prophecies?" he asked

"I do not know. I am a Roman slave. I cannot enter their minds. I do not have the Jewish feeling for things and for events."

Herod grew angry. The anger surged through him like molten lava.

"I have established peace in this province. I have restored order and brought prosperity. Yet I am hated. They plot against me. They carry this great hope of a Messiah. While they do I am in danger. Who can root it out? Tomorrow a shepherd bearing a crown may ride up from the end of my kingdom to Jerusalem and they will follow him because he is a Jew."

He walked about the room, trying to burn off his anger. Even in old age he could not control himself.

The merchants went to their inn to talk to their friends. They despised Herod, this man of mixed blood; a very mongrel in their eyes.

"We have opened the trade routes to Egypt. It is a good deal. In Jerusalem our warehouses will be protected. Herod can grant us security. Our goods will be safe."

"There is little else that matters. We will pay him his levy and shower gifts upon him. One of our family can come to Jerusalem and take care of the business. Jerusalem will become a key centre for our operation."

They felt proud of their wealth. Many years previously their grandfather had set out for Asia Minor as a copper-worker. He was a man of great ability and by his death he had set up the first family trade routes. Since then their business had expanded, their fortunes increased.

The inn was crowded but it had quiet rooms away from the noise of the street that the merchants occupied. Their servants attended to the merchants' wants. They had brought their precious carpets with them. They had set them out on the floor and upon the walls in order to bring colour and comfort to their surroundings. As the three brothers looked from the balcony to the courtyard below they noted the mass of people milling below them. They disliked such closeness to ordinary people but it could not be helped. The census was a blessing in disguise. It had given them an opportunity to open the Jerusalem trade routes.

They barely noticed the tall man who arrived that evening through the northern gate, leading a donkey upon which a young woman rode. He was tall and broad-shouldered, a man perhaps of twenty-five. His cloak fell easily down his muscular body. The dust of the road was on his hair and face and robe. He wore rough leather sandals. He found a quiet corner and turned to the young woman on the donkey. Her face was slightly concealed by her cloak. She was pregnant. It was obvious that she should not have been on the road at all. But Caesar had to be obeyed while the Romans ruled the world.

The man lifted the woman from the donkey. He set her down on a seat. "Our journey is almost at an end. Another day and we will reach Bethlehem. We will rest in some inn or other and you will be taken care of."

He spoke with a northern accent. He belonged to the province of Galilee and had spent many days on the road. The couple had passed through Samaria. It was said that it was a hostile place but both he and his wife had found hospitality amongst the poor. They stayed with a carpenter and the traveller, Joseph of Nazareth, had paid for his lodgings by giving the man a day's work. It was a fair exchange. They had spoken of the old rift between the Samarians and the rest of the Jews; it was a deep division but there seemed little sense to it.

"I felt the child stir within me," the woman said.

"Then you better rest. I will find a place for you," he said. He led her away from the noise and the bustle.

An old woman, who went each day to the temple, came out the shadows. She was dressed in a widow's clothes. She rented a small room at the inn. She had come from the north many years before after her husband had died.

"I will take care of your wife," she said quietly. "I have been praying in the temple and a voice spoke within me. I have waited for many years for such a voice."

Joseph of Nazareth left his wife in the care of the woman. She brought her to her room and set her down on the bed. She arranged her clothes and drew a heavy blanket over her against the winter cold of Jerusalem.

"Sleep now and I will recite the psalms of David."

The woman slept. The old woman looked at the fine skin of her visitor. It was without blemish. The young woman slept peacefully in the small room.

Next morning there was the usual bustle in the courtyard of the inn. Camel-drivers argued with each other over their camels. They had to be tackled. The great bales of merchandise had to be strapped on to their backs. It took some time to prepare the camel trains.

Joseph discovered that several of the merchants were on their way to Bethlehem. He could join their cavalcade.

His wife Mary was rested. Joseph had wondered if she should remain at the inn but the old woman who had taken care of her assured him that she was fit to travel. "I heard voices while I prayed. They told me that the child would be born in Bethlehem."

Joseph too had heard voices during the trying events of his life. With simple faith he had followed them as his forefathers had often done before.

The merchants from the north were eventually ready to move out of the inn. All that morning and well into the middle of the day warehouse-owners had been invited to their rooms to make tenders and the merchants wished to get the best bargain they could. It was important that the warehouses should be spacious and cool. Eventually they agreed upon two warehouses close to the northern gate. They settled the deals, sitting upon great cushions. The ease of their lives had made them soft and they could endure little physical hardship. They were men who made decisions while others did the physical work.

Finally it was time to depart. The camel train was ready in the yard. As their masters emerged, the camel drivers beat the camels until they knelt down. Then the merchants took their seats on the saddled humps. When they were ready they moved out into the bustle of Jerusalem. The camel boys pushed people out of the way. They felt very important as they moved through the milling crowds. Their masters from their high seats looked down at the torrents of humanity milling about them.

They passed out of the southern gate and headed for Bethlehem. Joseph and Mary attached themselves to the camel train with other working-class people. They spoke to each other in quiet voices. The merchants were indifferent to their existence. They spoke only of their wealth. They were descended from the royal household of David. A thousand years before he had been king of the land. His memory was as fresh in their minds as the events of yesterday. And it was prophesied that the next king would be born in Bethlehem. Perhaps one of their children might be the king. They could place their wealth at his disposal and he would lack no luxury. He would bear arms against the Romans and drive the invaders into the sea.

They spoke of these things as they passed down the road to Bethlehem.

The evening came. The air grew cold. The merchants called for their woollen cloaks. They threw them about their shoulders and wished that they were in the warm security of an inn.

The road passed over a low hill. From its crest they could see the roofs of Bethlehem. Here and there oil lamps glowed in the windows.

5

The Shepherds

Seth was the first to wake. His mother had already baked some bread in the clay oven and the room was filled with the pleasant smell. Daniel was hungry. It was strange to be lying in a bed in Bethlehem but he did not feel at all out of place. In fact he felt quite at home. Seth's mother treated him like one of the family.

He rose and put on his clothes. "Now you must both sit and eat. Seth sometimes goes without his breakfast. He'll stay small and thin if he does not eat properly."

Seth and Daniel sat at the table and and

Seth's mother handed them two large round cakes of the bread which she had baked. Following Seth's example, Daniel broke the bread and drank the milk which had been placed in front of him.

"Before you go down to the inn, you have to go up to the hills. You know that your uncle Jacob and the others are out minding the sheep. It is cold on the hillsides and I'm sure that they are perishing for want of food. Jacob cannot afford to lose his lambs so he has to keep a sharp look-out for wolves."

"I do not like going up to the hills with food," Seth complained. "It is always cold up there."

"You have no cause to complain. The Lord has been good to us. You have food to eat and you have shelter."

"But I have seen how the rich merchants live. I have seen them scatter handfuls of money among the poor. It is not fair."

As he was speaking his mother continued to place cheese and bread in a large sack. "You have to trust the Lord, Seth.

You have been told that at the synagogue."

"But I must trust myself, too," he insisted.

"You are impertinent. No more chat; you bring this food up to the hills *now*. I expect that Uncle Jacob is crying out with the hunger. You and Daniel should be able to carry a blanket each. It will keep out the cold on the night watches."

Seth twisted the neck of the sack into a rope and swung it on to his back. Daniel held it by the corner and eased the weight. They went out into the narrow street. It was cold and the sky was grey and low. The people of Bethlehem were dressed in their warmest clothes. The boys passed through the bazaar. There were many things for sale. A copper-worker stood surrounded by plates that he had fashioned as big as a soldiers' shields. Working with his punch and hammer he decorated the rim of a delicate pot. Further on, a jeweller was at work with fine wires of gold. They watched as he drew them into delicate shapes and soldered them to form a necklace. But the place which most attracted Seth was the food stall. Here were heaps of nuts and dates and sweets made from syrup and honey.

"No money; no sweets, Seth," said the vendor.

Seth lay down his sack and chased some money about the bottom of his cloak. It had fallen through the hole in his pocket. Eventually he drew out two small coins and presented them to the sweetseller.

The sweet seller looked at the coins. "Seth, what do you expect to get for such money?"

"Two bars of honey nuts. They last longest of all."

With a rueful smile the stall-keeper handed them the delicacies. The boys chewed them all the way through the bazaar and to the edge of the town. Here, olive trees grew in fields surrounded by stone walls. They were small and seemed very old and tired.

"A man's wealth is often judged by his olive grove," Seth explained. "Once my father owned many olive trees but he did not take care of them and they died. So my mother told me. He left us and never returned. My mother heard that he died in Jerusalem."

They continued up the gentle hills. Daniel noted that they were honeycombed with caves. He asked Seth if he had ever explored the caves.

"Oh, yes! But you have to be careful. They lead right into the hills and you could get lost there. But I know my way about. And in summer I often sleep in one of them, close to my uncle Jacob. That is when the pastures are green and deep. In winter the shepherds sleep in the cave when it is really cold. In fact my Uncle Jacob has a cave close to the town where he keeps his cow and donkey."

It was cold on the flanks of the hills. They moved up to where Jacob and the others had gathered about the mouth of a cave. The shepherds were sitting in a circle about a fire. Close at hand stood the flocks of sheep nibbling the meagre grass.

"Good morning, Seth," called Jacob. "How did you do last night at the inn with all the fine folk from out of town?"

"They were stingy with their money."

"Rich folk often are. Some love their money so much that they would love to be buried with it. But you cannot take your money with you. Now let us see what you have got here." He put his hand into the sack and drew out the food. He handed it to the others. Before they ate, Uncle Jacob called down a blessing on the food.

Uncle Jacob was a simple shepherd. His face was open and pleasant. He never complained about his hard and frugal life, not even when two years previously a wolf had killed many of his best sheep. His trust in the God of Israel was limitless.

"I have heard voices, Seth. They are not distinct but I have heard them. I tell you, something is stirring in these hills and it is something good. Some promise made a long time ago is going to be fulfilled. I heard a voice last night when I looked up at the stars and I declare that today I heard it again. There is a voice within my head. Something is coming. Something good is going to happen.

Seth and Daniel listened carefully to Jacob. Then soon it was time to leave the hills. "I'd better make my way to the inn," said Seth. "Ben will be looking for me. Ever since important people began to arrive at Bethlehem, he has little time for the poor or for his servants. He has lost the run of himself."

Seth and Daniel said goodbye to the shepherds, who were still huddled together about the fire. They descended the hill. There was a blue haze of winter smoke above the town of Bethlehem.

The boys could not resist another visit to the bazaar. It was much more crowded and filled with bustle and excitement. Sixtus, the Roman captain, stood at one corner keeping his eye on things. He had information that pickpockets had come from Jerusalem to prey on the visitors. He could not keep track of all the people thronging the town. The descendants of David seemed to be as numerous as the stars in the sky. He suddenly rushed through the crowd and caught an urchin by the back of his robe. He raised him up in the air as if he were a puppy. The urchin howled.

"Put me down. Put me down," he cried.

"Not until you have returned the purse you have just stolen."

"But I never stole a purse. I am just a poor boy."

With that Sixtus caught him by the feet and the hem of his robe and turned him upside down. The purse and some small loose coins fell from his pocket.

"Now you return the purse or you will end up in jail," Sixtus ordered him in his severest voice.

The urchin did as he was told and disappeared into the crowd.

Seth had always kept his distance from Sixtus. He was afraid of the man and knew his great powers. He could arrest anyone and send him in chains to Jerusalem.

Finally the boys reached the inn. "You are late," Ben roared. "I did not employ you to sleep late in the mornings."

"I had to carry food to my uncle Jacob up in the hills."

"I care nothing for your Uncle Jacob. There is much work to be attended to here," he said, and pointed to the kitchen.

They entered the kitchen. The fat maid-servant was sitting on a rickety stool. Seth thought that it might collapse under her weight.

"I'm beat out," she said. "This census has me worn to a frazzle. There is no end to visitors. Now go to the well and fetch water. And when you have done that, there are rooms to be swept and linen to be carried. So hurry up, the two of you."

It was one of those days when everybody was in vile humour. It began with the inn-keeper and he passed it on to his wife and she passed it on to the servants and they passed it on to Seth.

The boys took the brown water-jars and

went down the village to the well. As usual they had to wait their turn. They lowered the great wooden bucket down into the well and drew it up filled to the brim. They filled the jars and returned to the inn. Immediately they had to take besoms to clean out the empty rooms and prepare them for new visitors.

"We must eat," Seth said, and with that he went into the kitchen.

"We have no time to eat here," Liz told them.

"I have to eat and so has my friend. We work like camels and we are expected to live on thin air."

"Very well. Take some bread and dates. Eat them quickly behind the wine casks but don't let the master catch you. He is in a terrible mood and so is the mistress. She thinks that she is the only woman in Jerusalem who is expecting a baby. They believe that there will never be a child like their child. If you ask me, the child will be ugly."

They took the bread and dates and sat down to a comfortable meal behind the great wine jars. Seth enjoyed his food. They were barely finished when there was a roar from the corridor.

"Se-th. Se-th. More visitors," the innkeeper called.

Seth and Daniel rushed from the secret place in which they were hiding. There was confusion in the courtyard. Some merchants and rich people were departing. Others were arriving. A large caravan-train had arrived from the south. It was obvious from the condition of their camels and the richness of their clothes that the newcomers were rich people.

It was Seth's task to direct the camel drivers to their various stalls.

"This way. This way," he called, rushing about and directing the confused drivers. They were tired after their journey and quick to anger.

Eventually order was restored in the courtyard. The innkeeper was pleased. It was obvious that there would be a good night's takings.

"We're almost full," he told Seth. "We will have to turn people away unless they are very rich. Keep space only for the very rich."

It was growing cold now. The sky had been filled with menacing grey clouds. Now, in the evening, the first snowflakes fell like finest down. They were small and light but soon became heavier and thicker. The merchants demanded that fires should be lit in the courtyard.

Through the snow another group of caravans arrived from Jerusalem. The innkeeper and the two boys looked at the new arrivals. It was obvious that they were rich.

"We must make room for them," the innkeeper cried. "Soon the census will be over and business will slump again." He threw open the main gates. The snow was falling heavily and the camels and the figures were barely visible. The innkeeper held up a lantern and invited them to pass in. He noted that some poor travellers had tagged on to the end of the train.

"There is no room in this inn," Ben called. "Find lodgings elsewhere."

"But my wife is with child," said a tall man, who was leading a donkey. "Her labour has begun."

"That is no business of mine. Can't you see that I am full. You must find lodgings elsewhere. We must close the gates." And rubbing his hands in anticipation of his profit, he walked off.

Seth and Daniel looked at the man and the woman on the donkey.

"I can help you," Seth said. "Every house in Bethlehem is full. But my uncle Jacob has a cave. It is warm and dry. If you follow me I will bring you there."

Seth and Daniel closed the gates and set off through the blinding snow, the man followed them, leading the donkey which carried the woman. For some reason both Seth and Daniel felt happy and warm. They did not worry themselves about the anger of the innkeeper.

"You are kind boys," the man said. "Not many would go out of their way for us on a night like this."

At last they reached the cave. It was dark inside. But Seth with flint and dry straw lit a small fire at the mouth of the cave. He found an oil-lamp, trimmed it and soon there was light in the stable.

It was then that they noticed the woman. She looked at them with gentle eyes. Even the birth-pangs which were beginning did not cause strain on her face.

"I'll fetch my mother," Seth said. "She knows about new babies. She delivers most of the babies in Bethlehem. Come, Daniel. Let us hurry."

They rushed back through the narrow snow-covered alleyways until they reached his house.

"Hurry, mother. Hurry. A woman needs you. I put her and her husband in Jacob's cave. She is going to have a baby. There was nowhere for her to stay."

"You are a good lad, Seth," his mother said and, drawing on her cloak, she followed them through the blinding snow.

When they reached the cave, it was bathed in warm light which did not come either from the fire or from the lamp.

The man had hung a blanket across the cave to form a partition. The donkey and the cow, which were munching hay from a stall, brought warmth to the place. Outside the snowed had ceased to fall and the stars became sharp and bright.

The boys waited by the fire for an hour while their mother tended to the young woman. She cried out in labour only once and then they heard the cry of a child.

Very soon the curtain was taken down by Seth's mother. A child in swaddling clothes lay in its mother's arms. The tall man and the two children looked at the baby with its tightly shut eyes and red face. Seth's mother said it was a boy.

They did not know how long they stood there but they felt a deep peace in the cave and time was of no account.

Up in the hills, Uncle Jacob had watched the snow come out of a dark sky. He immediately set about calling his sheep together. They knew his voice. They quickly answered his call and gathered about him. Soon the other shepherds arrived with their flocks.

Just as the snow ceased to fall, Jacob heard voices in his head. He seemed to hear the lines of Micah:

> *But thou, Bethlehem Ephrathah,*
> *though thou be little among the*
> *thousands of Judah yet out of thee*
> *shall He come forth unto me that*
> *is to be ruler in Israel...*

He knew at that moment that the prophecy had been fulfilled.

"We have a journey to make to Bethlehem," he told the others. "We must bring gifts to a new king."

"But we are poor men. We have no

wealth," they objected.

"Take three of our best lambs. Place them on your shoulders and follow me. Two can remain on guard."

They did as they were ordered. They placed the lambs on their shoulders and followed Jacob down the snowy hills. The light in the cave showed them the way. Soon he stood at the entrance. He ordered the others to halt. He moved forward and knelt before the child. Then he ordered the shepherds to place the lambs on the straw.

"He is the promised one," Jacob said. "I have heard the voices and I know the prophecies."

The night passed cheerfully. Twice the mother fed the child. It was Jacob who decided that he should be placed in a manger. He took his sheepskin cloak and he laid it on the bed of straw. Then the child was placed in the crib. He slept peacefully.

Morning came. The countryside was covered with a deep carpet of snow. It was time for Seth and Daniel to return to the inn. They made their way through the quiet streets. When they entered by the small door, the innkeeper was waiting for them. His face was purple with anger.

"Where were you last night? Don't you know that the merchants had to be served? On the busiest night of the year you disappear into the snow. I have a good mind to fire you both. Where were you?"

"A woman's time had come. We directed her to a cave. Soon afterwards, her baby was born. My mother helped with the delivery."

He looked at them. "Very well. I'll forgive you this time. There is much work to be done, breakfasts to be prepared and rooms to be swept. So hasten to your business."

They quickly set about their work, yawning a little. It had been an exciting night.

6

Aleppo and the Roman World

The Magi rode out of the desert. They had followed the new star as it moved before them during their long journey. The sun was beginning to fill the bowl of sky. Everywhere lay ribbed sand dunes. The camels nodded their heads mechanically, never showing signs of tiredness, their great padded feet firm on the shifting sand.

Some of the servants had complained. Their lives at the observatories had been pleasant. They had the best of food to eat. Now their diet consisted of nuts and water. Their eyes, which had been filled with the rich colours of flowers and trees, now rested only on sand. Their ears, once filled with the music of birdsong, now heard only the crying of the wind that swept up sandstorms without warning.

Then they saw Aleppo. It was built on the very edge of the great desert on eight small hills and was surrounded by luxuriant palms. Among the palm trees stood finely wrought buildings.

"The most difficult part of our journey is over," Melchior said. "We have braved desert storms, encountered brigands and endured thirst to get here. Now we can rest for some time before deciding when we should move on."

"Let us move forward," Caspar ordered.

They set out on the last few miles. The harshness of the desert was left behind. They had come out of the wilderness.

What seemed to have been an oasis now turned out to be a fertile plain on the banks of a river. As they moved nearer they could see great caravans moving up from the south towards the city.

Finally they reached the outskirts of Aleppo. Among the trees they could make out fortified walls. Beyond the walls stood fortresses and temples. The Magi and their servants reached the southern gate. Roman soldiers stood on guard. A captain came forward and asked them whence they had come. Zenos, the chief servant, explained to him that they had journeyed across the desert.

"You are lucky. Not many survive. It marks the limit of our empire to the east. Several brigands have tried to make their way across the desert to escape the justice of the Roman law. Not many make it to the other side."

He enquired of their business in Aleppo. He was impressed when he heard that they had come to study the stars above the city. They explained that they were astronomers and had an interest in the heavens.

He passed down the line of camels and cast an eye over each servant. He had been trained to detect spies and enemies. He looked each servant in the eye. "Very well," he directed. "Carry on." The soldiers guarding the gate stood aside and they entered through its great arch. They were astonished by the architecture of Aleppo. Great Roman arches carried an aqueduct across the city. From the aqueduct, water flowed into stone basins. The chief street was straight and wide. On each side traders had set up their shops. They were opulent places filled with merchandise from many countries.

People from all over the known world were to be found in the streets of Aleppo. There were fair-skinned traders from the far north and others from even more distant lands with yellow skin and slanted eyes, who had carried silk across the great silk roads. There were traders from Greece with olive faces. There were sea captains and sailors who had travelled to the end of the Black Sea.

Everything could be bought and sold in Aleppo: slaves from the north; corn from Egypt; bitumen from Petra; purple dye from the south; horses from Byzantium. Here in the shops behind the colonnades, business was done quietly and secretly.

The Magi and their train moved along the main thoroughfare and came to a Roman temple where statues to the Roman gods stood in alcoves. The Magi observed all this great activity with interest. The Roman Empire seemed to be as rich as they had been told. It had an order and was well policed by soldiers.

Soon Zenos discovered an inn where they could rest. It was a comfortable place, built about a paved courtyard in which water from a three-tiered fountain splashed into a great marble basin. The Magi were weary after their journey. They bathed in a great domed room. Their muscles were eased by their servants and the tension massaged from their bodies. Then, putting on their finest silk robes, they sat before the great fountain and ate a light meal of wheat cakes, grapes and pomegranates, dates and other fruits and drank fine wine.

They talked of many things as they sat in

the courtyard at Aleppo. They had seen much and were able to add certain stars which they had not noted before in the western sky to their charts and give them names. Then their sacred texts were read and they listened intently to the scriptures.

As they sat in prayer a Roman, dressed in a toga, entered the courtyard. He moved with grace. He waited until the devotions were finished. Then he stood before the Magi and bowed to them.

"You are welcome to Aleppo and the protection of Rome. Severus the legate wishes you to visit him at his villa. He has heard that you have come from the east and he would like to meet you. Perhaps you would dine with him this very evening."

"Very well. It would indeed be our pleasure, " Balthasar told him.

When the messenger departed, they considered their position. Should they tell Severus of their mission. Would the fact that they were following a star which they believed would lead them to a king offend the Roman official? Perhaps the great emperor at Rome would also be offended. Perhaps the conversation might not turn in that direction. They were now in Roman territory and they believed that they would receive protection.

"We must trust in this star which directs us," Melchior said. "So far we have passed through dangerous places without harm."

It was a sensible decision. They were far from their country. Their servants, though armed, could not fight off a determined enemy. They needed the power of the star to protect them.

Evening fell over the beautiful town of Aleppo. Lanterns were lit at street corners. The merchants and the craftsmen returned to their mansions and quarters. Roman guards walked through the streets and a double guard was set on the great gates.

Litters were sent for the Magi. They were carried through the town to the walled palace. The doors were thrown open and within stood the villa of the legate. It had been built in the Roman manner with pillars and arches. A mosaic pattern had been laid down on the courtyard. It mirrored the lamps as they moved across to the villa. They passed up paved steps and entered a great hall in which a small fountain played. A meal had been set out for them. Great couches were arranged about a table which was set with the finest dishes of fruit.

Severus came to meet them. He was dressed in a white toga of the finest wool. On his feet he wore sandals.

"You are welcome to my villa. One of my guards told me that you had come from the east across the great desert and I was most anxious to meet you. Pray be seated."

With a refined gesture of his hand he indicated where they should sit. He noted that Balthasar was the oldest of the Magi and he offered him the couch nearest to him. When they were comfortable, he took his place and ordered his servants to bring them silver dishes of fruit.

The legate's hair was cropped and grey.

His face was taut and lined and he looked older than his years.

He inquired about their journey. Then with an educated ease he began to speak of the stars. He asked them for the names of their constellations. He in turn gave them the Roman names for the stars. He was a man of some knowledge in these matters and they did not notice the time pass.

"You have noted the new star," he said.

"Yes. Some months ago it appeared in the east," Melchior replied. "In fact Caspar, here, observed its birth from one of our watchtowers."

"Does it bode good or evil for the world?" Severus enquired, looking carefully at them. The eyes of Caspar and those of Severus were locked together. The magus could not escape the other man's penetrating gaze.

"We believe it foretells the birth of a king."

"A king to challenge the emperor?"

"We believe not," Balthasar answered frankly. "We cannot look into the future but we believe that it bodes well for the human race. Perhaps he may be a king but he will also be a priest."

"To night it rests above Aleppo. Where will it set?"

"We do not know, but we intend to follow it."

"You are fortunate men who can take time to follow a star. I must remain in this city by order of my general."

Severus was a cultivated man. His mind turned to other subjects. He was interested in the country from which the Magi had come.

They explained that their country consisted of great fertile plains. It was watered by canals and crops and fruit grew easily under a kind sun.

"Some day I will return to my farm in Etruria. There I will cultivate the land as I have always wished. On the plains I will set corn and wheat, on the lower slopes of the hills I will plant vines and on the high summits trees. It is a life I have often thought about as I marched to do battle with some enemy of my country.

Severus spoke knowingly of land. His feeling for it was real and he knew the qualities of the earth and what would grow on chalky earth, or on fine dark earth or on stubborn stony earth. He spoke with great affection of his youth in Etruria of his travels through the world.

The Magi found his conversation engaging. He had looked upon stars that they had never seen. He was a moderate man and drank light wine in measured quantities. It was towards the end of the meal that a woman servant approached him. She was agitated. He listened to her carefully.

"It is the fever, my lord. His body is on fire and I fear that he may die. He has worsened during the day."

"I am afraid I must leave you," he said with great courtesy. "My young son is far from well. Some strange fever burns within him. I will have my servants accompany you back to your inn."

"May we see the child?" asked Balthasar.

"We carry herbs and medicines with us from the east. Perhaps they may be of some benefit."

He considered their offer for a moment. "Very well. Come with me."

They followed him down a corridor to a room where a young boy lay on a bed. He was sweating heavily and his clothes were drenched with perspiration. He cried out feverishly. His mother and two women sat by the bed and dried the sweat from his forehead.

The wise men approached and looked at the boy. Balthasar felt his forehead and his pulse. The boy's heart was racing. He called his servant and directed him to go to the inn and bring his chest of medicine. When it arrived he took some herbs and powder which had been given to him on the way and had them softened in warm wine. Then he raised the young boy's head and made him drink the wine. Soon the child was in a deep sleep. Balthasar ordered blankets to be brought and placed over the body.

"Do not change the blankets. He will sweat out the fever during the night. With the sweat the poison will be drawn from his system. He will not awake or cry out. I have given him a sleeping potion along with other herbs."

The Magi returned to the inn and prepared to sleep.

Next morning there was a loud knocking on their doors. "Come quickly. The legate wishes you to visit him."

They dressed quickly and returned to the villa. They were escorted to the sick-room. The boy was still asleep but his body heat had fallen. The blankets were drenched with sweat. Balthasar placed the palm of his hand on his forehead.

"Tomorrow he will be better. He will be weak for some days but soon he will be playing with his friends."

"The star brought you here and with the star came your knowledge of herbs," said Severus. "Had you not arrived my son might perhaps have died. How can I thank you?"

"We seek no thanks," said Caspar. "We enjoyed your hospitality and you shared your knowledge with us."

They were invited to stay at the villa for the day. In the library they studied charts of the heavens which the legate owned. That night they were again invited to be guests at an evening meal. It was during the meal that news was brought that the young boy had woken from his sleep. They rushed to the bedroom and it was obvious that the fever had passed. The legate's son smiled weakly and spoke in a whisper. Balthasar prepared another sleeping potion. Soon the boy was asleep again.

Before they left the villa the legate invited them to drink a toast with him. Amber wine was brought from a cool cellar and poured into golden cups.

"This wine is from Thrace. It is celebrated by Homer, the Greek poet, as the best wine in the world. I drink it only on special occasions. Let me toast your journey south for I perceive that the new star is moving towards Judea and you must follow it. I wish I could travel with you. But you will be under my protection until you reach Jerusalem. Three of my soldiers will ride with you to the gates of that city."

They thanked him for his kindness and returned to their inn. The next day they set out on the road to Damascus.

7

The Enrolment

It was intended that the census would take ten days. It was hoped that everyone would by then have returned to their place of origin to register their names. All over Judea people were on the move.

A secretary had arrived at Bethlehem. He was a pompous man named Qualitas. He had thin features and a large domed forehead. He arrived with a servant, Felix, who carried his parchments, ink and writing-equipment. He hired a house in the town and set about preparing for the registration. All over the Roman empire, secretaries were preparing to do the same thing. He visited the best houses in Bethlehem, where he was received hospitably. Many people considered themselves privileged to have the Roman gentleman in their company.

"People are easily impressed," said Seth's mother, when she heard that Qualitas had visited a neighbour's house. "I'm sure she had out her best ware and he ate the finest food which could be purchased at the marketplace. She is the very one who complains about the price of everything. Next month she will not have a crust."

It took Qualitas three days to prepare for the census. He made out posters in ornamental script and had them pasted up in all public places. For those who could not read he employed a bell-ringer to travel from street to street announcing that the census would take place. Ezra, the man with the loudest voice in Bethlehem, was employed as crier for the census. Qualitas trained him for two hours before he had his lines correct.

Time and again he had to cry out: "By

order of the great Emperor Augustus of Rome a census will be taken of the citizens of Bethlehem during the last days of the month. Not to register on these days is tantamount to civil disobedience and subject to heavy fines by Qualitas, appointee of the Emperor Augustus and directed to carry out this important task."

All day, Ezra travelled through Bethlehem making the announcement. Soon everybody knew the lines by heart.

"Enough, Ezra," the merchants said. "You thunder in our ears. We know what you have to say."

"I have been appointed by Qualitas to carry out this order and I must obey."

The night before the census began, Bethlehem was filled with visitors. The population had doubled and the innkeeper, in an attempt to make as much money as he possibly could, put people in his barn and in the lofts. On the evening of the census, Ben doubled his prices. When people protested he said, "If you feel that you cannot pay, then sleep in the open fields or in the caves. My inn is new and well-heated, and we give an excellent service."

People were packed into every nook and corner. Some even slept in the corridors and only the rich were permitted to enter the courtyard where the great fires burned.

That night, Felix made his appearance at the inn. As there would be queues of people standing outside the census office he let it be known that for a small bribe he could make sure that merchants and rich people would not have to wait in line. He could have their names quickly inscribed on the register.

The next morning, Seth and Daniel arrived early at the inn. They were immediately set to work. All day they carried food from the market, fed the camels, brought wine to the merchants and the rich and attended to all the other chores.

"He is working us to the bone, Seth," Daniel complained.

"I know, but where else can I find work in Bethlehem? I have to bring home a wage to keep us in food."

But at midday they took a break from their work. Liz, the fat pantry-maid, had heard of the birth of the child in the cave. There was a whisper in the kitchen that the new-born child was of great significance. The shepherds had carried him gifts and others had made their way to the cave to pay their respects to the child's mother. She was a woman with a quiet and reserved manner who accepted the gifts of the poor with dignity.

"Make sure the child is warm," the servant-woman told Seth when she heard they were to visit the cave. "Take this blanket and give it to her. And bring her this bread."

The boys slipped out a side entrance and rushed through the streets and along the path to the cave. Joseph had built a fire at the entrance and it kept out the bitter cold. The baby was asleep in the manger when they arrived. They presented their gifts to Mary.

"You are very kind," she told them in her musical voice. "And blessings will follow you to the very end of your days."

"Did the child sleep well last night?" Seth asked. "I heard wolves howling and I wondered if he was afraid."

"He slept well. And the heat from the animals kept him warm."

"The census begins tomorrow. It will be a cold day and you may stay at our house when you come to Bethlehem. If you stand in the long queue you could catch cold. My mother has invited you to stay with us. You can leave the baby with her while you register your names."

Their ears ringing with the couple's thanks, Seth and Daniel left the warm cave. Even at midday it was cold outside. The skies were grey and a cold wind came off the hills. Their teeth chattered as they returned to the inn. Only inside and close to the fire did they felt comfortable.

It was late when they left the inn that night. Every space was occupied and so people wished to register their names as quickly as possible and leave Bethlehem. The census was very expensive for the poor.

Next morning the snow was falling silently on the town. It was unusual to witness such a sight in Bethlehem.

At dawn the people in the inn began to stir. The poor ate the parcels of food they had carried with them. Then, having paid the innkeepers, they slipped out the side entrance and made their way to the census office. Qualitas had not yet opened the door. They formed a long file outside. Bethlehem was only-half awake.

Eventually the door of the census office was opened. Felix, wrapped in a Roman cloak, appeared at the door.

"If you can write inscribe your name, family name, employment and place of origin, on the census form. If not, reply to the questions which will be put to you. Make your answers brief. Thank you. Census about to begin."

The census queue, running like a thread through Bethlehem, moved very slowly. A baker's boy moved along the line tempting people with rolls of bread warm from the oven.

At midday one of the merchants emerged from the inn. He walked directly past the long queue to where Felix was waiting for him.

"Come right along sir," Felix said, bowing in a fawning manner. "You are expected."

"It is unfair," one of the men cried as he watched the merchant stride past. "We are all descendants of David."

"You may be, but some descendants are more important than others," Felix replied venomously.

And so it continued through a single day. The poor waited and the merchants were given preference. They were now too cold to complain.

At sunset the census office closed down.

"Qualitas is weary. He must rest and eat. His mind is taxed with numbers and names," Felix said. "Come back tomorrow. We will continue as long as it is necessary."

The cold line at the census office broke. People were chilled to the bone. Grumbling amongst themselves they returned to the inns and the squalid quarters which the inn-keepers had made ready for them.

They were never permitted to enter the courtyard. It would be another night of misery for them in the dark corners of the inn.

For Seth and Daniel it was another busy night. It was very late when they left Ben's inn by the side door. They were too cold and tired to visit the cave. However, the next day, Joseph and Mary, as they had learned to call the Nazarenes, and the new infant would stay at the house and prepare for the census.

The cold continued. On the hills the shepherds kept watch over their sheep. The wolves were becoming very hungry with the cold weather. Each night they approached nearer to the sheepfolds. If a sheep broke free it was instantly set upon and dragged into the hills. Each morning the shepherds gathered in the new-born lambs. This year, after the birth of the child in the cave their flocks seemed to thrive. Jacob believed that the new child had brought blessings upon them. He recited the psalms of David in thanksgiving for his good fortune.

Next day, when the light was strong in the sky and the cold not so deep, Joseph and Mary and the infant made their way to the house of Seth's mother. She had prepared a special feast for the new-born child. They sat about a table and, following an old custom, she gave Seth and Daniel sweetened bread and honey along with some dates she had purchased at the market. They stood about the baby. He was full-faced and content and had a pleasant expression.

Seth left the house and went down to the census office. The queue was short so he returned and told Mary and Joseph that they could register their names.

He led them through the warren of streets and brought them to the census queue. While they stood in line a prosperous merchant passed by and entered the census office. He was illiterate and had to call out his name. He called it out loudly and took the opportunity to claim that he was directly descended from King David. When he was finished he marched out, accompanied by Felix who returned with him to the main door of the inn.

And finally Joseph and Mary were ready to register their names. They stood before Qualitas, who did not look at them. He was too busy studying his nails. Then he took his pen and asked:

"Can you write?"

"No," Joseph replied.

"Names."

"Joseph and Mary," Joseph answered.

"Children."

"A new-born child."

"Male or female?"

"Male."

"Name?"

"Jesus."

"Place of residence?"

"Nazareth."

"Occupation?"

"Carpenter."

"Good day. Next please."

Their census duty was finished. They left the room and made their way back to Seth's house. It was warm there and they sat about the oven in which Seth's mother baked bread. They spoke of many things and they did not feel the day pass.

"Soon you will present the child in the temple," Seth's mother said.

"Yes, in a few days' time. We would like to stay in Bethlehem for a while. When the child is strong enough we will return to Nazareth. The weather at present is too cold and the journey too long," Mary replied.

"Then you are free to remain with us."

"No. The cave is quite comfortable. We have no wish to disturb you. We will be quite all right," Mary replied.

"Could we go with Joseph and Mary to Jerusalem, mother?" Seth enquired. "The census is almost over and there will be little work at the inn for the moment. I would love to visit the sacred city."

His mother was about to refuse him but Joseph said, "He has taken care of us during the last few days. Now I will take care of him. Seth and Daniel would both enjoy the sights of Jerusalem."

The boys could not believe their good fortune.

Two days later, when the snows were melting and a warm wind blew from the south, they made the journey along the road to Jerusalem. They were very excited. The child Jesus would be presented in the temple. Seth knew the history of the holy city from the Bible and he related the story to Daniel as they walked along. It had been in the power of the Jessubites and bore the name Jebus when the Israelites arrived in the promised land. David had made it a royal city. Nebuchadnezzar later conquered it and almost destroyed it.

When the Israelites had returned from captivity in Babylon they had set about restoring it. Now it was occupied by the

Romans and Herod had built himself a palace there. Seth mentioned the name of Herod with a tremor of fear in his voice. He was a wicked man. He had even killed his own children to protect his throne.

They entered the city from the south through a gate close to Herod's palace. They looked at the king's strong fortress. Soldiers stood on guard. They scrutinised everyone who entered.

When the company reached an open square Joseph told Seth and Daniel that he and Mary must now go to the temple and present the child to the Lord. If they wished they could explore the city and meet them later.

They immediately set out through the winding streets. Their eyes widened at the great number of people who crowded the narrow bazaars. They had never seen so many shops and things for sale in their lives. There were carpets from Persia, silks from China and a bear from Turkey. His owner stood beside him in a small square while the bear danced for a circle of people. Elsewhere a magician made a copper cup disappear from before their eyes and made it reappear out of an old man's satchel.

They bought some sweets at a stall and then drifted down a dark lane. It led into a small courtyard. It was a place of shadows and they were afraid. The place was full of rough voices. The men who sat at the tables looked dangerous. They were drinking heavy red wine and they carried swords. Many of them had evil faces.

"You got no business here," a servant-woman told them. "These are Herod's blackguards. They do his evil work for him. They would cut out your tongues as soon as look at you. Come with me quickly."

She brought them through a series of underground rooms and up a secret stair. It opened on to the bazaar.

"Now on your way," she told them and banged the door. They breathed a sigh of relief. They had enough of adventures in the old quarter of the city. They decided that it was time to visit the temple.

They had heard much about Herod's temple, the most splendid building in Jerusalem. It was a place sacred to the Jews, built of vast stone blocks. It stood above the city, perched on a rock. The sun caught its turrets and it seemed to glow like gold.

As they ascended the first set of steps they noted how the merchants had set up their stalls. Everywhere they were selling souvenirs of the temple. The more expensive ones were models of the temple cut from marble, and there were several seven-branch candlesticks on sale. There were also money-changers. In front of them lay boxes of foreign currencies. They haggled with travellers over the exchange rate.

"Do you wish to beggar me. I give a fair rate of exchange. You visit any other money-changer in Jerusalem and you will not do better. I am an honest man."

"No moneylender is an honest man," the irritated pilgrim said. "I did not come all the way from Greece to be robbed in

Jerusalem. The pagan Greeks are more honest than some Jews I can name."

"Seek your change elsewhere. I will not do business with you."

They were still eating their sweets as they mounted further towards the temple. They passed beyond the court of the gentiles. Any gentile who passed beyond this court could be put to death. They entered the court of the women. They were about to advance further when an old woman who was kneeling in prayer called out to them.

"Stop eating your sweets. You are on holy ground. If the high priest were to see you, you'd be whipped with leather thongs."

The boys quickly hid their sweets and advanced further into the sacred place. Here they could smell incense. There was an air of quiet. Old men with beards and glorious robes chanted prayers. They knelt down and Seth recited some of the psalms of David. Then, tired of the prayers and the heavy incense, they made their way out of the temple proper and into the court of the gentiles. Here there was much excitement. They began to eat their sweets again.

In the meantime, Joseph and Mary had made their way to the temple to present their first-born, Jesus. They had purchased two doves, the accepted offering of the poor, to sacrifice for the occasion. As they entered the temple with several other parents, an old man came towards them. His eyes seemed filled with some inner light. His name was Simeon and he had made the temple the centre of his life. Each day he spent many hours praying there.

"May I take the child in my arms?" he asked simply.

Mary handed him the child. He looked at the small features in awe.

"I have waited for this moment for many years," he said. "No day passed but I did not pray that I would cradle him in my arms. This child is the saviour of all people and will be a light to the gentiles."

He held him for some time. Then he

handed him back to Mary. He bowed and passed into the temple. There were tears in his eyes.

The same thing was to happen as they left the temple. An old prophetess named Anna also took the child in her arms. She was eighty-four years of age and she lived close to the temple.

Joseph and Mary met Seth and Daniel as they had arranged. They sat on a stone bench and ate some simple food and observed the crowd. Then the boys set out on their journey to Bethlehem.

It was almost dark when they reached the quiet town. Most of the visitors had left the place and it had returned to the activity of ordinary life.

Daniel knew that something terrible was about to happen. However, he could not tell his good friend Seth.

8

Damascus to Jerusalem

The Magi took the trade route to Damascus, which lay directly south. It was a journey of over two hundred miles. They joined a large caravan coming from Asia Minor and travelled through a mountainous region. To the west lay tall serrated hills that ran like a spine through the land. The higher mountains were covered with brilliant snow that sparkled in the sunlight.

The long string of camels followed the trading routes which had been used for a thousand years. Alexander the Great had passed along this road on his way to Babylon.

The Magi were becoming used to the Roman world. It was notably different to the civilisation from which they had come. The buildings and forts along the route had been constructed by the Romans' best military engineers. The roofs rested on arches and pillars. Statues of Roman gods were set on pedestals and in niches in the outer walls. In their temples the westerners offered incense to many gods. Melchior, Caspar and Balthasar worshipped a single god who had created the world and held it protectively above the blackness of chaos.

The first evening they stayed at a fort that had been built beside the caravan trail. It was a grim place, made of mud and straw which had hardened under the sun. Four towers stood at the corners of the rough building. To the east the sand stretched to the horizon. On the western slopes of the mountains they could see cultivation. Vines clung to the lower slopes and higher up the mountain and below the snow line the great cedars grew, tall and majestic.

The star which they had followed glowed firmly in the south. They wondered if it would lead them down to the very ends of the world, which lay below Egypt at the mysterious sources of the Nile.

Their servants found them a comfortable room in the garrison. Here they laid out rich carpets and marked off a quiet corner where they might worship. As the night fell over the desert they prayed before a lamp which carried a steady flame to their god. Then they recited their ancient psalms.

Outside they could hear the Roman soldiers singing rough barrack songs. They had carried wine from Aleppo and they now opened the great pitchers. They were tired of the desert and wished to return to their homes in Italy.

When the Magi left the small enclosure they noted that a great fire burned in the centre of the barrack square. A merchant from the north had arrived while they prayed in their room. He was dressed in the rough sheepskin clothing of the mountains. He drank with the Romans. In a huddle close by sat a boy and a girl. They were white-skinned and blond-haired. Their eyes were filled with fear.

Zenos, who knew many languages, began to talk with them. "Where do you come from?" he asked.

"From the great mountains. We lived in a quiet village where we herded sheep. Then the slavers attacked us. They killed our parents and sold us into slavery. There were many of us. We have been purchased by Retzor. He believes that we will fetch a high price in Egypt because of our fair skin."

While they were speaking, Retzor broke away from the Roman soldiers.

"You dance for us," he cried catching the girl and boy by the hair and drawing them into the circle.

The children stood staring at the soldiers.

"They are animals and as dumb as oxen," Retzor said to the soldiers. He took his whip and brought it down on their backs.

"Dance," he ordered, "or I will flay you alive."

He would have whipped them but a voice on the outer circle of the fire said, "Leave them be. They are afraid." It was the voice of Balthasar. He moved into the light. He was dressed in his priestly robes and his face was calm and dignified. The Roman soldiers who had been sent to accompany him stood close by. Retzor looked angrily at this intruder from the east.

"They are mine to do with what I like. If I wish I could slit their throats and could not be blamed."

"How much would they fetch in your market?" Balthasar asked.

"Fifty gold coins."

"Then I will purchase them for fifty gold coins." Balthasar said.

There was silence about the camp.

"It is a fair deal," one of the Roman soldiers called drunkenly. "Accept the offer and buy wine for the company."

"I have to consider the offer. Perhaps I

could get sixty gold coins in Alexandria," Retzor said, his eyes filled with greed.

"Alexandria is far away," a Roman soldier reminded him. "You'll have to feed them on the journey. It could cost you heavily to bring them so far."

Retzor became cautious. He should have done the deal quietly. The Roman soldiers were ruthless. He would have to be careful with his money.

"I'll sell," he said taking the two slaves to where Balthasar stood. He offered the chains to the magus.

"Set them free," Balthasar ordered. "Those who serve me are not bound to me with chains but with affection and respect."

The links were broken and the boy and girl came forwards to where the tall magus stood. He placed his hands on their heads and gave them his blessing. Then he gave them into the care of Zenos.

Retzor returned to the Roman soldiers.

"You are a rich man now, Retzor. Let us play dice," one of the soldiers suggested.

"I do not gamble," he said.

"We shall teach you," they laughed.

One of them took two bone dice from a purse. He shook them in his hand and spilled them on to the sand.

The numbers amounted to three.

"Surely Retzor can beat such a small number," they said.

He took the dice and shook them in his hands. He threw them on to the ground. The numbers came to eight. He won a gold coin.

He continued to win. He ordered wine for the soldiers. It was late into the night when fate turned against him. He noted that he was losing heavily.

"I will play no more," he said. "I must sleep. I am drunk."

The soldiers whipped out their daggers and pointed them at his neck.

"You will play until the sun rises," they said.

All night they placed dice. Twice the throw favoured Retzor, but his luck did not hold good. By morning he had lost his fifty gold coins. In a final bid to retrieve his fortune he bid his camels on a wager. He would win everything or lose everything on the final cast of the dice. The dawn was breaking on the horizon when he cast the last dice and lost everything. Drunk, he staggered to his bed and fell asleep.

Next morning the Magi left the sinister barracks with their servants and the two freed slaves. They knew that further south they could encounter the new king.

It took them some days to reach Damascus. Like the other cities and stations along the trade route, it had seen the comings and the goings of traders for a thousand years. The weather was warm during the day but at evening they had to wrap themselves in heavy cloaks against the chill. They had set out at the end of spring and had gone through a summer and a spring on the journey. Many of the servants who had come with them wondered if their mission was a fruitless task. They too had seen the star rise in the east and they had been filled with excitement. Now the excitement had given way to home-sickness. They wished that they could return to their pleasant rivers, where the land was fertile and life less arduous.

The Roman soldiers came with them to the gates of Damascus. Before they took their leave, the Magi gave them the gold coins as they had agreed. They thanked them, saluted, mounted their horses and rode north.

Lines of apricot trees marked the approach to Damascus. It was one of the oldest towns in the world and it was close to the kingdom of Herod. It was surrounded by orchards and gardens and the air was filled with a heavy fragrance even during the short winter season. The Magi understood why it had a hundred poetic names. After a journey through arid land it was pleasant to look upon.

Zenos immediately went in search of comfortable quarters for his masters. The Magi proceeded along the street called Straight. The street had been set out when Alexander the Great conquered the territory.

It was almost a mile long and wide enough for chariots and people to move freely along its route. Much trade came through Damascus. The Jews, the Greeks, the Romans and others had set up agencies here. It was said that a hundred different gods were worshipped in this densely populated city. The Magi took a great interest in all these matters. They would have much to report to their friends in the east when the journey was over.

They settled in for the night in a pleasant inn. It was while they were praying that Melchior heard a voice in his mind. He knew then that their journey was almost over. Soon they would reach the palace of the new-born king.

9

The Meeting

Janus, Herod's secretary, made his way along the palace corridor. It was early morning and he had not slept very well. He was a man who normally required little sleep or food. He had nibbled at some fruit as he watched the dawn break in the east. His stomach was tight with worry. Herod was a difficult master. The palace was filled with intrigue. Nobody's life was safe, not even his own. It was difficult to survive in the household of Herod the Great.

"Blood, blood and more blood. His life has been a river of blood. There is no one whom he trusts any more. He has executed his wife and his sons. He has tortured men until he has extracted the very secrets of their souls."

When Janus recalled the deeds that had been done in the dungeons of Herod's palace his flesh began to crawl. Herod had always used violence and terror to hold on to his power. He always feared conspiracy against him. Now in old age he had become suspicious of everyone and he listened to the dark whispers of informers who fed his hunger for secrets. His spies were everywhere, in the palace, in the streets, in the towns he had built, in the small villages far from the capital.

"I will have no mercy on those who conspire against me," he declared to Janus when he felt his position challenged. "All my life I have defended my throne. Queen Cleopatra tried to destroy me and she is dead. She even persuaded Antony to give her my finest property, the balsam gardens and palm groves of Jericho. A most dangerous lady, full of intrigue, but now she is in her tomb. I have had to fight for every inch of my kingdom. No one will take it from me. Not an acre, not a rood..."

Two nights previously Janus had had word of a conspiracy against Herod. Certain young Jews had met in a house in the old quarters. They were zealots who observed the Jewish law to its last detail. They wished to purify the land of its Roman poison and restore the kingdom of Israel. They had decided to assassinate Herod when he visited Caesarea, a town he had built from its very foundations. It had theatres, temples, aqueducts, storehouses and public baths.

They had been seized as they left the house. Now they were in chains in the dungeon. Herod had not yet been informed. Janus would immediately have told his master, but a servant woman who had worked for his wife for many years had come to him and pleaded for her son's life.

He had considered the position carefully. The previous evening he had visited the dungeon, examined the young men and ordered them to be set free.

If Herod had discovered that he had intervened his life would be in danger. This thought was uppermost in his mind as he passed through the corridors.

Already the palace was beginning to waken. Servant women were sweeping the mosaic floors. The clerks were preparing for the days work. Several people who sought an audience with Herod were already in the courtyard.

He knocked at the door and entered. Herod was good-humoured on this particular morning. He was pleased with the contract he had made with the merchants from the north. The trade routes were filling his coffers with gold. The money he would invest in the construction of fine buildings. He would not be satisfied 'till he had made Jerusalem a Roman city.

"Well, Janus, what business have we to deal with this morning?"

"Some letters have arrived from Rome. They are of no importance. The stewards have come from your estates in the south. They bring with them the accounts for the last year. Indeed your lands have been most fruitful. They wish to present you with a white stallion they have reared for you."

"Good. Any man who serves me well will be rewarded. Call them and I will go over the accounts."

He stood at the window and looked west at the great temple he had built for his people. It glowed in the morning light.

Janus was right. Herod was in good humour. Yet Janus knew that he could quickly grow angry. He placed the open letters on his table and went in search of the foremen. He could not but wonder what the day might bring.

In the meantime the Magi approached Jerusalem. They kept the Sea of Galilee and the Jordan to the west until they reached the old town of Jericho. Here there was a fertile oasis. They were tired of the dusty route they had travelled. Soon they would rest in the shade of the palm fronds and have a proper meal.

The two slaves whom Balthasar had freed were now dressed in clean robes. Their hair had been washed and trimmed and the fear had left their eyes. Already they were picking up phrases of the language spoken by the followers of the Magi.

Zenos consulted with the Magi.

"Jerusalem is close at hand. I will set out and find you lodgings for the night. As we seem close to the birthplace of the king it is wise that we spend a few days in the city and prepare to meet him." He set out for Jerusalem.

The Magi and their retinue slept during the middle of the day. They were wrapped in their warmest blankets. Later they set out for the sacred city. That evening they entered the city by the north gate. Everywhere they looked they could see the hand of King Herod. The buildings were magnificent, particularly the temple.

Their inn was close to Herod's new

palace. It was an opulent place and it was private. They rode in through the gates, which immediately were closed again. The innkeeper had his servants attend to the needs of the travellers. It was obvious to him that these were important people, perhaps some type of nobility. Because his inn was close to Herod's palace many important visitors stayed with him while they awaited an audience with Herod.

"And where have your noble masters come from?" he asked, making no attempt to conceal his curiosity.

"From the East, beyond the great desert," Zenos told him.

"Then you are not the subjects of Caesar?"

"No."

"And what, may I ask, brings you to Jerusalem?"

"We have come to pay homage to the new king."

"But Herod is our king. He has been on the throne for many years."

"No, not Herod. But a new king that is born or may soon be born."

The innkeeper questioned no further. He knew the politics of Jerusalem. He went indoor and called his wife.

"They come to pay their respects to a new king. They say a king has been born. What shall I do?"

"Tell Janus. You know that you have been warned to pass on every important piece of information you hear in the inn," she told him.

"Then tonight I will visit Janus. In the meantime I must return and administer to the wants of these travellers. It is obvious that they are very wealthy people."

He was a small fat man with protruding eyes and a large nose. He was interested only in making a fortune. Someday he would be an important person in Jerusalem, recognised for his wealth and position both by the priests and the Romans. He would be pointed out when he swept into the temple with his gifts.

He moved among the Magi and their

followers, trying to listen to their conversation. It was obvious from what one of their servants told him that they did not understand the political situation in Jerusalem. A stone's throw from where they talked was the most ruthless king in the Roman empire.

When they were settled in and had said their evening prayers the Magi decided to pay a visit to the Israelite temple. The innkeeper advised them not to go beyond the court of the gentiles. If they passed beyond that limit they would be in danger of their lives.

Accompanied by their servants, they made their way to the temple. They approached it from the south and moved into the royal portico. Monolithic columns with Corinthian capitals stood in four rows and supported the upper structure. Here were several stalls selling temple souvenirs. They mounted the steps and stood in the court of the gentiles. In the centre was the temple proper. It was still not complete. Even as they moved forward they could hear the noise of mallets and chisels dressing the great square blocks.

"Some day it will be finished. Then the Jews will have the finest temple in the world," a local guide told them.

While they stood gazing at the temple, several priests came forward to meet them. Already they had heard of the arrival of the Magi and their quest for a new king. News quickly passed through the streets of Jerusalem.

"You are welcome to Jerusalem," they said.

"We come in search of information," Caspar replied. "We have followed a star that rose in the east. We believe that it leads us to a new-born king. We have come to pay him homage."

The priests looked at each other fearfully. Perhaps they should not talk with these strangers. Already there was a rebellious buzz running through Jerusalem. Everybody knew the prophecies. They had learned them by heart as children and as young men they had sat at the feet of the rabbis and questioned them about the promises made to the prophets.

"Such a thing is prophesied in our books," they told the Magi.

"Tell us more," Caspar insisted.

"Perhaps you should inquire from the chief priests and the scholars. They know much more about these matters than we do. We are but simple men," they replied, and with that they hastened away and were lost in the crowds.

The Magi and their followers felt uneasy. Clearly, Jerusalem was not a place certain of its destiny. They had brought wonderful news to the city and it was not welcome.

"This is a strange city," they said to the guide. "It is obvious that the priests do not wish to hear our good news."

"They fear Herod. He lives in the palace close by." He pointed to a tower overlooking the great courtyard of the temple. "Often he stands and looks down upon Jerusalem. People fear him. He will not welcome the news of the new king."

It was dark now and the great court of the gentiles was almost empty. Pilgrims had begun to make their way back to their quarters within the walls of the city.

The Magi and their retinue decided to return to the inn.

That night as they slept, the innkeeper made his way through the streets to Janus. He had much to tell him. He knocked on a side door and was ordered to enter.

Janus was sitting in his small room reading a Latin scroll. It was the time of night, with Jerusalem at peace and Herod in his bed, when he could relax with a glass of wine and read from his favourite authors.

"I have told you that I do not wish to be disturbed at this time of night," he upbraided the innkeeper who stood before him with bowed head. "You had better have information of great importance."

"I do. I do," he said.

"Then tell me what it is," Janus ordered. The innkeeper, still with bowed head, told him all that had passed during the evening at the inn.

"You say that they seek a new king?"

"Yes. They speak openly about it."

"And what else have you to tell me?"

"Every Jew in Jerusalem is now speaking about it. They quote the prophecies. They say that perhaps this king will drive the Romans and Herod from the kingdom. Perhaps another David or a Solomon has risen amongst us."

Janus looked at the innkeeper.

He had lived more than twenty years in Jerusalem and he still did not understand the Jewish mind. The Jews had no wish to belong to the Roman world, despite the peace and wealth which Herod had brought to the land and the city.

"And why do they believe in such a thing? The Roman empire stretches for a thousand miles to the west and a thousand miles to the north. No force can disturb the peace. Can they not get it into their stupid Jewish brains that no king born can challenge the power of Caesar and no upstart dethrone Herod?"

"I know all these things, Janus. But you try and tell that to the priests and the ordinary people. I come only to tell you what I hear."

"Very well. I shall consider what you have said. Here is something for you. The information you bring is always useful."

He gave the innkeeper some coins and ordered him to leave.

Janus had lost his taste for wine and his Latin authors. He had a political problem on his hands and he must solve it before the night was out. He knew that words could flame into action. The Jews could rise up if their imaginations were fuelled by this news.

However, there was one advantage to be gleaned from the event. The fact that he had released three young Jews from the dungeon would go unnoticed.

He summoned one of his servants. "Wake up the high priests and bring them to my house immediately. I wish to speak to them on a matter of urgency."

He padded up and down while he awaited their arrival. They answered the summons quickly. Janus did not approve of them as a group. They were proud and pompous and they were always a threat to the power of Herod. However, they held high religious positions in the city and must be humoured. Above all, they knew that texts of the sacred books thoroughly and they could give him advice.

"Well, gentlemen," he began when they were seated. "I have a problem for you to solve. I am not familiar with your language or with your sacred books but I do respect them. Now it has been brought to my notice that wise men from the east have arrived in the city. They say that they come to give honour to a new-born king. The city is stirring with this news. Has a new king been born and what lies behind the whispers?"

For a moment the high priests were silent. Not one of these men wished to talk. They were holding back something. Janus looked at the impassive faces, half-hidden by long beards. He grew angry.

"Answer me," he said angrily. "You know something that is important to me."

"One cannot be certain. One can never be certain…" one of them began.

"Be certain of what? Answer me."

"The prophecies."

Janus looked at them. "Translate the prophecies for me," he ordered.

The chief began to recite in Latin: "Bethlehem in the land of Judea, you are by no means the least of the cities of Judea; for from you will come a leader who will guide my people Israel."

Janus considered the words. Words and ideas were his trade.

"You say leader, not king. Is he a leader or a king?"

"The texts are difficult to understand," one hedged.

"I wish to understand them and certainly Herod will wish the same in the morning. So clear your minds and give me precise answers."

"It is difficult to give such answers. The new king may be a king like David. Others believe that his kingdom will be a heavenly one. There are as many answers as there are wise men."

"What do the ordinary Jews think?"

"They believe that a king will be born who will rule this kingdom."

Janus considered the situation. He must inform Herod at cockcrow.

"Tomorrow morning at the break of dawn I wish to see you at the palace. I want you to tell Herod exactly what you told me. Good night, gentlemen."

They left the house of Janus and returned home.

"Ah, Janus. You must see my fine horse," Herod said when his secretary arrived the next morning. "There is no horse like him in all Judea. I will have him tackled to my chariot and drive through the city. But why the serious face? Are you ever cheerful?"

"I am cheerful when I bring good news.

This morning is not a morning for cheerful news. The city is buzzing with gossip and rumours."

"It always is."

"Three wise men have arrived from the east. They wish to worship a king."

"Then send them into my presence and let them worship me. I would like to be worshipped."

"You do not understand your majesty. This is a king newly born. They believe that he will save the nation. The diehards and the zealots say that he will push the Romans into the sea."

Herod's countenance changed. Fury flared in his mind. His face grew red with anger. He roared at Janus. "Where did such rumours begin? Is there any foundation to the whispers?"

"Last evening at the inn. They were started by the wise men. The do not understand the political situation here. But the rumour quickly spread through the city. People speak of it at corners and on the temple steps. I assembled the high priests last night. They tell me that a king is foretold in their sacred books."

"Bring them into my presence immediately. This rumour must be stifled. It could start a rebellion."

The high priests were shown into Herod's office. They were white with fear.

"Now, gentlemen, we have known each other for many years. I have been more than generous to you. If you have enjoyed your exalted positions it is because I, Herod, have seen to it and granted you favours. What is behind these rumours?"

He listened attentively to what they said. His anger was controlled. His shrewd mind began to work coldly on what they said. They were devious men and he had to look behind their minds and words. When they were finished he dismissed them and summoned Janus.

"These priests are tricksters," he began. "If they cannot explain a simple passage clearly to Herod then they must have the ordinary man's mind addled."

He paced the floor and considered his position.

"These wise men may understand the stars but they do not understand the politics of Jerusalem. They are men innocent in the ways of the world. I will have them visit me and I will speak to them. I will have them explain to me what brought them this far. Then we will understand more clearly what all this is about and can take swift action."

At midday news was sent to the Magi that Herod wished to honour them. He invited them to his palace. As he sat on his throne he watched them approach across the mosaic floor. He was impressed by their demeanour. He knew aristocracy when he saw it and these wise men moved in a princely manner.

Janus bowed to Herod and introduced Melchior, Caspar and Balthasar. Herod indicated that they should sit in seats close to him. He was a perfect host. He inquired about their journey and the kingdom from which they came. They were almost seduced by his charm.

"And this king that you have come to worship—could you tell me more about him? It would indeed be a great privilege to pay homage to one whose birth has been foretold by the stars. No star shone at the birth of Caesar. You can see why I am anxious to meet him."

Balthasar spoke for the others. He explained how their priestly cult had studied the stars for a thousand years. They had set their calendars by the stars. Crops were planted when the stars occupied certain places in the heavens and were harvested when they stood at other places. The birth of a new star in the sky, which had been mapped for a thousand years, indicated the birth of a king.

"And will you know when you have found him?"

"The star will no longer move through the heavens. It will stop above the place where he is born."

"And do you know the name of the place

where this will happen?"

"No. That has not been made known to us."

"I am indeed delighted that you came to Jerusalem. Go and search carefully for the child and when you find him let me know so that I may go and worship him."

The audience was over. The Magi presented Herod with precious stones and left the palace.

Herod stood alone at the window and looked over his city. No upstart king would take it from him.

Janus returned.

"What action should we take?" he asked Herod.

"None for the moment. Perhaps they may pass out of the kingdom and travel on to Egypt. I want them followed. In the meantime start another rumour in the city. You are good at that type of thing. Have it announced that they came to do worship to Herod. Let it be known that they brought me magnificent presents."

Janus left the room.

Herod wondered if he would ever have peace. Would his throne ever be secure from his enemies?

10

The Magi at the Stable

The census was finished. Qualitas and his assistant packed their documents and their bags and returned to Jerusalem. Sixtus, the Roman captain, was happy that the excitement was over. Several pickpockets had arrived from Jerusalem and caused him much distress. There had always been a few petty thieves in Bethlehem but they were known to him. The Jerusalem pickpockets were professionals and difficult to catch.

"I'm delighted that it is all over," he told the innkeeper as he stopped at the great inn on his rounds.

"Not me," the sad-faced innkeeper replied. "Business was never better. The census brought money into the place. Now we must depend on the odd merchant who passes through."

"How is your new baby?" Sixtus asked.

"He cries a lot and keeps his mother awake at night but he is healthy and strong," he answered proudly. "I have looked forward to this child for many a day. He will own this inn and all my wealth and he will take care of me in my old age."

"I hear that there have been many births in Bethlehem during the last two years. The population is growing. There will not be enough room for them at the synagogue if all this continues."

Bethlehem was a quiet town again. People returned to their daily round of work. The shepherds remained on the hills taking good care of their sheep. The rabbi taught at the synagogue and the women chatted at the well each day as they went to draw water. They were very critical in their remarks about the innkeeper. He had become haughty and proud during the census. He had turned poor people away from the comfort of his inn.

"The cave was no place for this woman Mary to have her baby," one began as she lowered the bucket into the well. "She is such a quiet and refined young woman. If it had been the wife of some merchant she would have received total attention. A cave was good enough for her because she was poor. But the infant Jesus is healthy. I called on her last night. They refuse to leave the cave for the moment. They find it quite comfortable."

"It is always the same. The poor suffer in this world."

"Did you hear what happened at the temple in Jerusalem?"

"No."

"Well a neighbour told me. Apparently an old priestess called Anna came and took the child in her arms and said that he had a great future. So did an old man who had been told in a vision that the child was special."

"In what way special?"

"I'm not certain. But he said great things were in store for him. And did not Jacob the shepherd hear voices up in the hills?"

"And there was a whisper in the houses that the child Jesus may perhaps become a king."

"There is something about that family which suggests good breeding," Seth's mother remarked. "I would not be surprised to hear that they were direct descendants of David."

Seth and Daniel were aware of the child's importance from the very beginning. Every day they visited the cave to see if there was anything they could do for the young woman and her child. When they were finished in the inn they climbed up into the hills to speak with Jacob. Sometimes they stood watch over his sheep while he returned to Bethlehem for a rest. The sheep were tame and gathered fearlessly about them. When they walked to a new pasture they followed them obediently in a group, the small lambs frisking on the edges of the herd. Seth and

Daniel were protective of the lambs. They could stray into a gully and get lost, and there was always the threat of hungry wolves.

When they returned to the inn to see if there was some work they could do, Gideon the gatekeeper was anxious about the child Jesus. "The cold weather is over so there is no danger that he will catch cold but one can never be certain with children. They pick up all types of illness. You can't be too careful. You know I have been recalling passages from the sacred books. Did you know that a king will be born in Bethlehem?"

"No," they replied.

"Well, it is stated in the books. Perhaps this is the child. It certainly is not Ben's child. I never heard a child kick up such a fuss in my life. Cries all night. And the mother will spoil him. He will be just like his father. He has his big head."

When the two boys left, the old door-keeper's face grew dark. He knew the prophecy concerning the king but he could also recall a prophecy from Jeremiah and the words frightened him. He hoped that he might be mistaken but his mind was filled with fear.

He was about to take his seat by the gate when the innkeeper came down the stairs and across the courtyard where he was sitting.

"Any visitors passing by?" Ben inquired.

"I'm afraid not, master. There has been little call for accommodation since the census was taken," he replied.

"You should be out on the street watching. I do not pay you to sit all day on this seat. You are getting old. If you are not up to the work I will get a younger man." The old man bowed his head.

Night was falling over Bethlehem. The sky was filled with stars. One star in particular seemed to glow warmer and brighter than all the rest. It moved across the night sky. Jacob was aware of its presence on the hills, as was Gideon. They had not seen such a star before. Clearly, it was of some significance. Both quickly realised that it was something to do with the child who had been born in the cave. There could be no other reason for such a wonder.

Seth and Daniel were the first to see the Magi. They entered the town by the Jerusalem road. They rode on camels and it was obvious from the harness and the leather that they were people of importance. Seth and Daniel immediately walked beside the camel train. There were twenty camels in all and a great number of servants. In the centre rode three men. They were serious faced and majestic. They looked towards the sky at the star.

"Where are we?" they asked

"Bethlehem," Seth told them.

They looked at the sky. Everybody in the camel train was looking at the sky. Suddenly the star stopped. It began to pulse warmly as if it possessed an excited heart.

"It has stopped," they said. "The star has stopped. We have arrived."

Seth looked at Daniel.

"What are they talking about?" he asked.

"The star. Look at the star. It is shining above the cave."

Immediately the Magi ordered the camel train to stop.

"We must ride no further. Let us walk," Balthasar ordered. "Our journey is at an end. Prepare the gifts and have them ready."

Still looking at the star they passed through Bethlehem.

The innkeeper, when he saw them coming, rushed on to the street and almost threw himself under the feet of the camels.

"I have the best accommodation in Bethlehem. I can promise you food and heat and comfort. I have the finest wines in the land in my cellar and the best and rarest food in my larder," he called.

But the company was in a trance. They moved past him, their eyes still on the star. They left the town and moved towards the cave. Now the star had finally stopped.

The Magi took the gifts from their servants. Holding the gifts of gold, frankincense and myrrh in their hands they moved forward to the mouth of the cave. At the entrance to the cave they knelt down and bowed to the woman and the child. They stood motionless for some minutes. Then Balthasar moved forward and placed his gifts at the foot of the child's manger. He was followed by Melchior and then by Caspar.

They entered the cave and for two hours they talked with the mother. Their company stood at a respectful distance.

Nobody knew what the Magi said to the lady. But it was obvious that they were happy in the presence of the child. Then when the conversation was finished they withdrew, bowed reverently and permitted the rest of the retinue to approach the cave. Each person laid some small gift at the infant's feet.

They parted as quietly as they had arrived. They did not stay at the inn. Instead they pitched their tents some distance from the cave and prepared for the night.

Herod's spy watched all that had passed from some distance. He was confused. He had been told to follow they camel train and discover where the Magi were bound. They had stopped in front of a shepherd's cave and presented gifts to a poor child. It did not make sense.

He quickly returned to the inn. The inn-keeper was in a dark mood.

"What brings you here?" he asked.

"I have been sent by Herod and I have to ask some questions. Who is that child in the cave?"

"I have no idea. He belongs to some poor family. He was born some time ago. His father is a carpenter, I believe. They could not afford to stay at my inn."

"Is the child royal?" he asked.

"Royal!" the inn keeper laughed in scorn. "Royal. Now I know royalty when I see it. They certainly are not royalty. Royals come from the upper class."

The spy decided to stay in Bethlehem. He had been ordered to keep a close eye on the Magi.

That night the Magi sat together and

talked. They felt that their lives were now complete, that some mystical experience had visited them. They knew the purpose of the star and they knew why the child had been born in a stable and not in a palace. He could bring about a new order and his influence would be benign. He would not bear a sword but he would be a new voice in the land. They agreed that they would return to Herod and explain the message of the star.

But that night Balthasar had a disturbing vision. He cried out in the darkness of his tent and his servant, who slept close by, came to visit him.

"Quickly. Order the camels to be harnessed. Pass among the servants and order them to prepare to move. We must leave as soon as possible. Make as little noise as you can."

"Will we return to Jerusalem?"

"No. We will return to our own lands by another route."

While the preparations were made under the supervision of Zenos, Balthasar put on his royal robes. He left his tent and returned to the cave. There he sat with Mary and Joseph and spoke to them for an hour. In a final gesture he placed his hands his hand on the forehead of the infant, pronounced a blessing and left the cave. When he returned to the camp it had been broken and they were prepared to move. He mounted his camel and ordered them to move south. They must continue south for two days and nights before they could pitch their next camp.

The star which they had followed for many months disappeared from the sky.

11

Massacre

The spy woke next morning. He went up to the balcony of the inn and looked towards the cave. Already Joseph had started a fire. Smoke drifted quietly towards the slight hills. The sky was clear and the air mild. The cold weather in Bethlehem had definitely passed.

He looked everywhere for the wise men. They seemed to have disappeared.

The spy feared for his life.

He rushed down the stairs and out the main door into the street. He looked up and down. The place was almost empty. Nothing was happening. He hastened down the main street and came to the bazaar. An old man with one eye was setting up a small stove on which he baked unleavened bread. He was poking the small fire into life when the spy roared at him.

"You!"

The old one-eyed man looked around and focused his good eye on the spy.

"Me?" he asked.

"Yes. You. Did you see a camel train pass by on its way to Jerusalem?"

"No."

"Did you notice anything strange this morning?"

"No."

"Can you put two words together?"

"When I have to. Sometimes I put ten words together if it is very important. But most things are unimportant."

The conversation was becoming frustrating.

"Is there anybody in Bethlehem who can give me information?" the spy asked.

"No. They are all asleep. They are late risers in Bethlehem."

The old man continued to poke the fire. The spy turned away from the frustrating little man.

He would have abandoned his quest for information and returned to the inn but he heard the sound of a donkey coming from the south. He waited for the rider to approach. He hoped that he would have more to say than the old one-eyed man.

"Excuse me. Did you happen to notice a camel train as you travelled north?"

"Indeed I did. It is many miles south by now. The people moved at a great speed and they refused to tell me where they were going."

"In what direction were they moving?"

"Egypt. But they could easily swing east and travel across the desert."

The spy was in a quandary.

He returned to the inn and began to think. Ben tried to engage him in conversation but he snapped at him. Finally he decided upon a course of action. He would remain in Bethlehem for the day, return to Jerusalem that night, and say that he had followed the Magi south. Having ascertained that they were going to cross the great desert, he decided to wait a little longer in Bethlehem.

When Bethlehem did awake, the women make their way to the well for water and gossip. They had all heard of the visit of the wise men. Furthermore they had heard that the young woman, Mary, had received rich gifts.

"Strange that princes should come all the way from the east to pay their respects to the child," one woman remarked.

"There is more to this than meets the eye. He must be a child of some importance. Clearly we do not know the whole story," said another.

When the servant woman, Liz, returned to the inn she was full of the chat. Ben heard her talking with the other women.

"What do you mean by a chest of gold,"

he queried.

"I am telling you what I heard. They left the child a chest of gold. The coins bear the image of some eastern king."

Ben was confused. He would not understand why eastern princes should camp beside a cave and not spend a night in his comfortable inn. He was also angry. His newborn child was the most important child born in Bethlehem and nobody had brought him a shekel.

"Imagine that," he told the spy. "Three eastern princes visit Bethlehem. They carry gifts of gold to a carpenter's child. They camp beside a cave and next morning they disappear."

The man knew that this information would be vital to Herod. He had come in search of a new-born king and he had found him. Herod would never know that he had been sleeping when the wise men left the area.

That day, Seth and Daniel went out to the cave. Mary had fed the child and he was lying contented in his manger. Beside him stood gifts of gold, frankincense and myrrh.

The two boys looked at the chest of gold. It was a small ornamental box, with bronze hinges.

Mary could see their great interest in the box. She told them to open it and examine its contents. They did. They counted the coins. There were fifty in all.

"Now, I would like you do something for me but you must tell no one," she said in her soft voice.

"We are good at keeping secrets," Seth told her.

"I wish you to take the coins and give four each to the people who most need them in Bethlehem. People have been so kind to me and I wish to repay them."

"But what of yourself? You too need money," Daniel said.

"We will not lack." she told him.

Sitting on the straw Seth made out a list of twelve people to whom he would give the coins. His mother was on the list as well as the door-keeper at the inn.

"We depart tomorrow for Nazareth so you can distribute the gold tonight," Mary told them.

"Very well, lady. I will do what you command," Seth told her. "But what will I do with the remaining coins?"

"Keep one for yourself and give one to your friend Daniel."

"We will miss you when you leave," Seth told her.

"Some day you may pass through Nazareth. Call to see us. I predict that you will become a merchant. You will travel to the ends of the earth and you will be a very rich man."

Seth and Daniel returned to Bethlehem. They spent the day between the bazaar and the inn. It was evening when they returned to the cave. They took the chest from Mary and slipped back into the town. From Seth's house they set about the task of distributing the money. It was very late when their work was finished. The door-keeper was the last one they visited.

They pressed the four pieces of gold into the palm of his hand.

"Mary sent it to you. It is to thank you for your kindness."

The old man looked at the gold pieces. They were worth more than he could earn in ten years. He no longer had to worry about Ben and his ill-temper. He could now buy a house and rent a small olive grove.

"I'm no longer at the bottom of the heap," he said.

Night came. The lights went out in the houses. The fire in front of the cave fell inwards and began to smoulder. It was at three o'clock that Joseph had a dream. He awoke from sleep and sat up. There was a cold sweat on his forehead.

"Mary," he called. "We must depart from this place and go south to Egypt. I have had a warning. We mustn't lose a moment."

Quickly Mary prepared for the departure. An hour later she, Joseph and the baby left the cave which had been their home and took the road south. A bright moon gave them plenty of light.

"What!" Herod roared when the spy brought him the news." The Magi gave their gifts to a child in a stable? Are you out of your mind?"

"I tell you it is true. They gave him gifts of gold, frankincense and myrrh. Then they fled south. I followed them at a distance."

"It cannot be such a child. He could not be king. They must have made a mistake. It is some other child. I tell you that it is some other child. Yet the gossip is that the new-born king has been born in Bethlehem. I will put an end to it."

His fury was as wild as a raging sea.

Murder was not new to Herod. It was a quick way to solve an immediate problem. He had killed his wife, he had killed his sons and now he would kill every child born in Bethlehem and its surroundings."

"Bring me Thebel. He is perhaps drinking in some tavern at this time of night. Tell him that Herod has work for him to do."

The servant sought him in the lowest quarter of Jerusalem. He feared for his life. Here every renegade in the city lived. He knew the reputation of Thebel. He carried out Herod's darkest commands without question.

He found him in a tavern drinking wine. He was drunk. About him sat his henchmen. Some were snoring loudly on the filthy floor.

"Thebel," the servant said. "Herod wishes to speak to you. He has urgent business which needs attending to."

Thebel shook himself. He looked through half-drunk eyes at the servant.

"I will visit him in the morning."

"He insists on seeing you immediately."

Thebel staggered to his feet. He was over six feet tall and had a brutal face and a rough body. He kicked his sleeping men awake.

"Herod has work for us. Be prepared," he said and staggered out of the tavern.

He was very drunk and the servant had to lead him to Herod's quarters. As always he approached by a secret entrance.

"I will speak to Herod alone," he said angrily to the servant. "I always speak to Herod alone." He pushed open the door and entered Herod's room. He knew the moods of the king and cared little for them. They had been associates for many years. Thebel had carried out the assassinations for Herod as far away as Rome and Egypt.

He went directly to a pitcher of wine and poured himself a goblet. He drank it quickly and wiped his mouth.

"It is much better than the wine in the tavern. What murderous work have you in mind for me on this night?" he asked.

"I wish to round up your men, ride quickly to Bethlehem and put every male child of two and under to the sword."

Thebel, though drunk, was taken aback.

"What? Has Herod descended to murdering children? Are you losing your mind in old age?"

Herod explained to him what had happened in the last few days.

"I know these people, Thebel. You know

them. Give them a whisper of a messiah who has come to save them and they will take up arms. The throne is under threat."

"It is dirty work. But you pay me well and I do not question your commands. But the men may not follow my orders."

"Here. Get them so drunk that they will not know what they do," Herod said, and slid a bag of gold across the table.

Thebel took the bag of gold and tossed it a few times in his hand. He could judge its value.

"Herod is generous," he said. "Herod must be very troubled." And with that he walked out the door.

He returned to the tavern. He ordered the most potent and expensive drink. Soon the men were drinking heavily. At four o'clock in the morning their minds were dull and their tongues loose.

"We have a mission to accomplish. It must be done quickly. We should have finished our work by eleven and be back here at twelve if we ride quickly enough. Now let me tell you the nature of the mission."

He explained to them what they had to do.

"If you have no stomach for this work, then stay here. If you do that you will no longer be a soldier of mine."

They staggered drunkenly out of the tavern and made their way to the stables. Already Thebel had ordered a servant to harness the horses. The men mounted awkwardly. As the dawn rose over Jerusalem they rode out of the city.

The sharp air sobered them slightly. They rode in ragged formation, twenty men in all. They were the riff-raff of the Roman army, all of them professional killers.

It was eight o'clock when they reached the hill above Bethlehem. They looked down on the town. It had one main road running through it.

"Gallus," Thebel directed. "Take ten men and approach the town from the south. We will approach it from the north. Every house must be searched. Every child of two years and under must be put to the sword. These are Herod's orders."

Gallus took his men and moved them along the crest of the hill and took up their positions at the south entrance to the town. Thebel waited till they were ready. Then his men formed a line. They began to move menacingly and with purpose towards the town.

What happened in the next hour was engraved on the memories of the people of Bethlehem for countless generations. The horsemen scoured the streets. They banged upon doors and woke people who were sleeping. These cried in panic when they saw the soldiers. Gallus broke down the first door. Inside a family lay sleeping on the floor, a father and mother and three children. He whipped the clothes from the children's bed, judged that one of them was under two years of age, took it by the hair and carried it screaming into the road. There in front of his men he plunged his sword through its small body. He held the impaled child over his head.

"First blood," he roared. The soldiers jumped off their horses and moved in a mad fever through the the streets. Women cried out in anguish as their children were torn from them, killed and thrown like useless dolls on the ground. A cry went up from the town.

Sixtus heard the wailing. He quickly put on his leather tunic and his sword. He rushed on to the street.

He watched in horror as a child was slaughtered before his eyes. Drawing his sword he rushed towards the soldier.

"I represent Roman order in this town!" he called.

"And I am Herod's man," the soldier replied. Sixtus engaged him with his sword. He would have killed him but Gallus charged Sixtus with his lance. It pierced the leather jerkin and sank deep into his body. With a quick turn of his wrist he withdrew it. Sixtus fell dead on the road.

Ben the innkeeper tried to hide his child but a rider burst through the main door of the inn and entered the courtyard. Ben cried out, "Kill me but not my child."

"We did not come to kill the old but the young," the killer roared, snatching the child from the father's hands. Holding the screaming infant above his head he rode out of the inn.

Ben followed him. "My child! My child!" he called in despair.

Before his eyes the soldier drew his sword and ran the child through the heart. Blood instantly flowed from the small mouth. The soldier threw the dead child at Ben.

"There is your precious child," he called.

There was death and confusion in the small town of Bethlehem. Slaughter continued through the morning.

Seth and Daniel looked at the bloodshed from a side street. They were trembling with fear. They did not know which way to run. They feared the rough soldiers, who were mad with bloodlust.

"Quickly. Let us run along here," Seth said.

They rushed into a small street and began

to run as quickly as they could. And then they heard the thunder of horses' hoofs. They looked about. The soldier was bearing down upon them. Seth turned into a side street. Daniel continued to run forward, his feet turning to jelly. The soldier raised his sword to bring it down upon him. Daniel cried out in despair. Then there was darkness.

Epilogue

The frost was deep. It had penetrated the earth and made it hard as iron. The grass on the green was grey and sharp like fine steel strands. On the windows of houses and cars the frost formed into fans and shells of delicate beauty. The streetlamps glowed softly in the cold air, a frosted halo about them.

Lights were going off in the village. One light still burned in the carpenter's shop. He began to choose his best planks of oak. The body of Daniel was certain to be discovered. He had given up hope of finding him alive and decided to make the coffin.

Daniel had disappeared on Christmas Eve. The townspeople had searched all the woods and fields near the town. Day after day they had combed the undergrowth. They had dragged the river. Their efforts had been futile. Hope had burned like candles in the windows for many days. Now as they penetrated deeper into January hope was quenched.

Soon John would take down the crib. Piece by piece, figure by figure, it would be carried to the back of his shed and stored.

"Next birthday he would have been ten," he said to himself as he placed the seasoned boards on his bench. With his eye he measured them. They would fit easily into their sad place when they were cut.

Suddenly, he noted how cold the shed was. He took some dry shavings and put them in the billy stove. He lit them and then threw small blocks on top of them. Soon the place was warm again.

He took up the first plank of timber and fixed it in the vice. He took his saw and was about to begin to cut it, but he had to lay it down again. He could not make the coffin. It was too final a gesture.

He decided to walk through the village. The sharp air would clear his head. Perhaps, afterwards, he might sleep. He had not slept for many nights. He threw some logs into the stove and shut the iron door. He wished that Daniel would appear, alive. He had loved the shop with its smells and colours and shapes and its secret dusty places.

"There is no end to sorrow," he said as he drew the door closed. He filled his lungs with sharp air. It cleared his mind. Putting his hands deep into his overalls pockets he walked towards the crib. The crust of frost crackled beneath his boots. As he moved towards the display he saw the figure lying in the pool of light. He ran forwards. Daniel, in a hooped position, lay on the ground. John bent down and listened. He was breathing deeply as if in a coma. He was about to shout and waken the village but he decided against it. He took the young boy, lifted him in his arms and carried him over to the warm workshop. He pushed open the door and carried him inside. He drew an old sofa in front of the billy stove and placed the boy upon it. He looked at the face. It was tense with terror.

He let him sleep. Soon the heat began to warm his body and he began to breath deeply and evenly. He stirred awake. He cried out. He threw up his hands upwards as if to ward off some danger.

Then he opened his eyes and looked about. Slowly it registered with him that he was in the workshop.

"Was it a dream?" he asked.

"Where were you, Daniel?"

"Bethlehem. I saw it all happen. I was there. It was wonderful until the soldiers came. They slaughtered all the infants. It all began the night I stepped into the crib. It came alive. I was there and I witnessed it all. I met the Virgin and Joseph and I held the child in my arms.

The carpenter knew that he had been through some strange experience. He decided to humour him.

"Of course you were there. But you must rest now. You are hungry and cold."

Then Daniel remembered. He felt in his pocket. Yes it was still there. He took out the gold coin and held it between thumb and finger. It glowed in the light.

"Look I have the coin. It was a gift from the Virgin. The Magi brought it as a gift to the young infant."

The carpenter took the coin and examined it. It was solid gold. It carried a king's image and lettering which he could not read. He went to one of the many old books which lay on a desk. He opened one and went through it. He compared it with an ink   drawing of a coin in the book. He held his breath. It matched a coin from a Chaldean kingdom. The book stated that only two such coins were in existence.

"Tell me about your experience," he said.

It took Daniel a long time to tell the story. John stopped him while he made tea in the old black pot that was furred with sediment.

Then when Daniel had eaten, he let him begin the story again. The carpenter knew that the story could not have been the work of the child's imagination. It was too accurate and too real.

"You have seen the wonder of the world," the carpenter said when he was finished.

"Do you believe me?"

"I do but others will not. Their minds are too dull. It would be better to say nothing about it. We know the truth and that is enough."

Next morning the carpenter told the village that Daniel was well. The people could not account for his disappearance and reappearance. His parents brought him home and he slept soundly.

That night in his room he heard movement and talk on the village green. He went to the window. They had taken down the crib surround. The figures stood alone on the grass. Then one by one and beginning with the wise men they were taken and carried across the green to the workshop. Soon only Sixtus remained. Then he too was taken and carried away. The doors of the workshop were closed and locked. The crowd dispersed.

Christmas had come to an end.

Also by Poolbeg

The Secret of Yellow Island

By

Mary Regan

*The spirits of the past have risen at last to
do battle with the spirit that is ageless –
the spirit of evil.*

When Eimear Kelly arrives in Donegal to
spend the summer with her eccentric granny
Nan Sweeney she is not prepared for the
adventure about to unfold.

Who is the frightening giant of a man Eimear
christens 'the Black Diver' who has rented her
gran's holiday cottage? What is his dark secret
and why is he poking about the deserted island
of Inishbwee?

When Eimear meets Ban Nolan, a mysterious old woman, and discovers the legend of
the Spanish sea captain, she is drawn into
many exciting and dangerous encounters.

The Secret of Yellow Island is a story of a
strange and unforgettable holiday.